WITCH'S FIRE

WITCH'S FIRE

Beverly Butler

COBBLEHILL BOOKS
Dutton   New York

Library of Congress Cataloging-in-Publication Data
Butler, Beverly.
Witch's fire / Beverly Butler.
p.   cm.
Summary: Thirteen-year-old Kirsty, confined to a wheelchair by a car
accident, finds herself living with a new stepmother and stepsister in a
strange old house formerly inhabited by a witch who wants it back.
ISBN 0-525-65132-2
[1. Witches—Fiction.   2. Stepfamilies—Fiction.   3. Physically handicapped
—Fiction.]   I. Title.
PZ7.B974Wi   1993   [Fic]—dc20   93-44   CIP   AC

Published in the United States by Cobblehill Books,
an affiliate of Dutton Children's Books,
a division of Penguin Books USA Inc.,
375 Hudson Street, New York, New York 10014

Printed in the United States of America
First Edition   10 9 8 7 6 5 4 3 2 1

To Betty Ren Wright Frederiksen
and for the entire personnel of Burning Kettle Acres
with sincere appreciation and deepest affection

1

THE FINAL two items in the suitcase on the bed were the photograph, carefully wrapped in layers of paper towel, and the thick green candle shaped like a Christmas tree.

Kirsty Hamilton lifted the candle out first, and sat cradling it in her lap while she searched for the best place to put it.

Not on the small desk, already crowded with her boom box and stack of favorite tapes. Not on the shelf under the desk where she couldn't see it.

She rolled her wheelchair to the dresser and centered the tree in front of the mirror. Perfect. It was doubled by its reflection, making a bold green accent in this otherwise blue and yellow bedroom.

Her sister, Gail, had given her this candle two Christmases ago, their last Christmas together. Gail had been thirteen then, and Kirsty eleven.

She pushed the memory away and returned to the suitcase. There was no question where the photograph would go.

"Maybe you'll want to keep this somewhere private," Grandma Pollard had suggested, helping her pack for today's journey to this old house in Wisconsin from the Florida condominium where her grandmother had been looking after her these past two years. "Keep it just for you."

Kirsty stood the photo in its silver frame squarely on the bedside table in plain sight. If it bothered her father's new wife, Rita, to see who the real Hamiltons were and how they had been, too bad for Rita.

The picture showed Kirsty's father and mother sitting together on a flowered couch. Gail leaned over the back, her fair hair almost indistinguishable from their mother's. Kirsty, dark-haired like their father, was perched somewhat askew on the arm. They were all four laughing because of Kirsty's last-minute scamper to get in position before the camera timer went off.

Who was sitting on that couch now, she wondered. What sort of people had bought it when the contents of that house were auctioned off?

Such a wave of homesickness struck her, she felt almost dizzy. If only there were some magic way to lift herself back into that picture. Back into that time when everything was so right.

She drew in her breath, squeezed her eyes shut, and clenched her fists, willing it to happen.

Slowly, the sounds beyond the closed bedroom door —the groan of a faucet in the kitchen, the murmur of TV in the living room—began to fade. She was floating—drifting—

A sneeze exploded behind her. Her wheelchair abruptly became solid reality once more.

A second sneeze, louder than the first, parted the blue-sprigged curtains hung across the opening of the closet. An orange tiger cat rocketed out onto the bed, sending paper toweling skittering to the floor.

Kirsty's startled "Hey!" launched him into space again. He landed on the dresser a whisker length short of knocking over the big green candle.

Kirsty doubled up coughing, a sting like smoke in her nose, and a stink like rotten eggs.

"Ugh! Go away," she choked. An ache jabbed behind her eyes like the tip of a probing finger. "Scat! Shoo! Get out."

The cat sneezed again, violently, and as if that ended the matter, sat down beside the candle to give his shoulder a quick, tidying lick. The candle rocked slightly.

"No! Get away. Scat!"

She clapped her hands at him, which made him crouch tighter to the candle as he turned his head to look at her. If she tried to grab him, he might knock it to the floor.

Perhaps if she opened the door he would leave by

himself. In any case, it would let some of the smell out and some sweeter air in.

She wheeled herself toward the door, but before she could reach the knob, it was twisted from the other side.

The door swung in, bringing with it Rita's nine-year-old daughter, Pam.

"Wow, it's dark in here," she observed as if she and Kirsty were old friends instead of strangers who had first laid eyes on one another only this afternoon. "Don't you want the light on?"

Without waiting for an answer, she flicked the wall switch.

Kirsty blinked, then frowned at the instant brightening of the yellow walls. If she hadn't noticed how fast the November dusk had been gathering in the corners, that was her concern.

"Don't you knock before you come crashing into a person's private room? This *is* my private room, isn't it?" Best to get the ground rules established right from the start.

"Sure, it's your room," Pam said agreeably. "We fixed it up for you specially because the other bedrooms are all upstairs. We even put curtains on the closet so you can get in easier than with a door." Her eyes, a pale sort of green, traveled curiously over Kirsty and the wheelchair.

"Super," Kirsty said, giving her a hard stare in return. This was without doubt the homeliest kid she had ever seen: tons of freckles on a pushed-in monkey face topped by rusty hair like a swatch of shag carpet.

Pam squirmed a little inside her baggy pink sweater. "Anyway, I could tell you weren't asleep, because I heard your radio on."

Kirsty had forgotten she was supposed to be taking a nap. Her father and Rita had felt she needed one after the stress of a day spent in and out of cars and planes and airports.

Once the door was shut between her and them, however, what she had needed most was to see things of her own set out in this magazine-perfect room where not one stick or thread resembled the room that she and Gail had shared.

"You didn't hear a radio. You heard my yelling at that smelly cat to keep away from my stuff."

"What smelly cat? Toby?"

At his name, the cat stood up and bunted his head against the candle, nudging it a fraction nearer the dresser's edge.

"Stop him," Kirsty cried. "Don't let him wreck that."

Pam's solution was to snatch the candle off the dresser.

"Hey, neat," she said, turning it over in her hands. "Is this a real candle? Can you light it?"

"No! Never! Put it back. Take that cat away from there." Kirsty nearly spilled herself from the chair in her lunge to rescue her treasure.

"Okay, okay." Pam sidestepped to escape her, and

5

shoved the candle toward the mirror. "Come on, Toby." She swept him into her arms. "How did he get in here, anyway? I thought he was upstairs on my bed."

"All I know is that he came flying out of the closet a minute ago like something was chasing him, and he made a horrible smell in there."

"Toby doesn't make smells in closets. He's a clean cat," Pam said indignantly. She set the cat on the floor, pushed the closet curtains apart, and breathed in half a dozen loud and lengthy sniffs.

"I don't smell anything. Only wallpaper and new paint. I don't see anything bad, either."

The smell was gone, Kirsty realized. The horrible smell had disappeared.

She rubbed her forehead where the ache had been, but the ache was gone, too, although there was a tender spot above her eyes like an old bruise.

"Well, I didn't make it up," she said, hating the idea of looking foolish to this Pam person. "There was a smell. Even the cat was sneezing from it."

"Toby? Poor Toby." Pam squatted to scratch him under the chin. "He acts funny in this house. Like sometimes he spits or growls and fluffs up his fur, or he sits and watches a wall but there's nothing there."

"Probably he hears mice," Kirsty said. It seemed altogether possible in an old house like this, despite its new paper and paint. Such a contrast to the bright and airy home she used to have.

"Cats don't growl at mice or act scared." Pam edged

up close to Kirsty's ear. "But know what it could be?" Through cupped hands, she whispered, "This house used to belong to a witch. A boy at school told me. She even tried to burn it down once so nobody else could live here. Maybe that smell was a witch smell."

The monkey face and the tone were so earnest that Kirsty felt a shiver crawl over her scalp in spite of herself. She pulled her chair back to regain a measure of space. "Aren't you supposed to go help your mother fix dinner or something?"

Pam grinned, no way offended. "We're having hot dogs, and we're going to let everybody roast their own in the fireplace. But Daddy said I could help build the fire when he's ready."

"Daddy?" For Kirsty, all other topics were immediately shelved. "You mean *my* daddy. He's my daddy, not yours."

"Sure, but I call him Daddy, too. He said I can call him anything I want"—Pam giggled—"except late to supper."

Kirsty's heart pinched shut for a beat. Her father had used that tired old late-to-supper line on her and Gail since she could remember. It was a family joke, private and personal, not just any old gag to throw away on outsiders.

"I thought you had a daddy of your own somewhere. What about him?"

"He won't care. He got married again and moved to Oregon."

7

"But you go stay with him sometimes, don't you?" Kirsty urged. She was hoping in terms of every school holiday and three-month summer vacations.

"Well—" Pam shrugged within her drooping sweater. "Oregon's pretty far to go. And it costs a lot." She drifted across the room to finger the collection of tapes on the desk. "Besides, my daddy doesn't relate to girls too much. He's got two little boys now, and they keep him busy."

So Pam's daddy was a nerd. Too bad. That didn't give her the right to claim Kirsty's. Kirsty was only just getting him back herself after two long years of separation.

He had been all that time "picking up the pieces," as Grandma Pollard put it. To Kirsty it had often seemed more like getting rid of what pieces were left: shipping her off to her grandmother as soon as she was well enough to travel; selling their house and possessions in Cleveland; leaving his telephone company job in Ohio for one hundreds of miles away in this northwoods town of Frederiksen, Wisconsin. And never once after the hospital ever mentioning to her either her mother or Gail. There had been times when she had wondered if the day might come when he would somehow forget all about her as well.

Then, three months ago he had phoned to tell her about Rita and that he planned to get married. He had promised they would be sending for Kirsty as soon as they found a house and were settled. Now here she was.

Only she hadn't come prepared to find everyone quite so settled as they appeared to be.

"What's it like to be in a car crash?" Pam asked suddenly. "Really scary, I bet." Kirsty's head came up. "What do you mean?" The accident was another subject she and her father never discussed.

"My mom told me—how this drunk guy slid through the red light and your mom and sister got killed. You and your mom and sister, you were driving home from shopping on a snowy night, right?"

A snowy night . . . If an image flickered in Kirsty's mind, it was too quickly gone to be grasped. What she remembered of that Saturday evening was tracking her mother through the throng of after-Christmas shoppers and giggling with Gail at a display of toilet paper stamped with beaming Santa faces. Next, she was flat in a hospital bed, fenced in by metal rails like the sides of a baby's crib, and there was a nurse who told her it was Tuesday.

Three whole days had dropped from her life without a ripple, taking with them her mother and her sister. And her home. She had gone from the hospital to a nursing home and on to Grandma Pollard's in Florida without ever setting eyes on her own house again.

She shifted the tall, broad candle to the exact center of the dresser where it belonged. "I guess you know as much about it as I do."

Behind her there was a long, considering pause. "Well—but now you've got a new sister. Me. And I've got a new sister. You."

"Sisters?" Shock roughened Kirsty's voice. She had never thought of such a thing. "No way. We're not sisters."

"Sure we are. Because now we have the same mom and daddy. They got married to each other, so that makes us sisters."

"It doesn't matter what your mom and my dad did," Kirsty said grimly. "You are your mother's kid and I am my dad's, and we are not any kind of way related."

In the mirror in front of her she saw the monkey face lengthen and lose some of its eagerness. "Anyway, we're stepsisters—"

The mirror also showed the photograph on the bedside table, and Gail's pixie face, as different from Pam's as a pansy from a potato. And that was nowhere near the whole difference. Gail was Gail. How could anyone suppose that she could be replaced?

"Stepsister means the same thing, that we're not related."

"Maybe my mom does want me to go fix supper," Pam said after a small silence. She brightened with a new idea. "Shall I push you out to the kitchen or somewhere?"

"No, thank you," Kirsty said. "I can get around fine by myself. I don't like being pushed."

One of the first things she had learned about wheelchairs was how to set the brake to avoid being at the mercy of officious chair-pushers who took control as if she were little more than a piece of furniture. One young man in particular—the physical therapist at the nursing home—had specialized in rushing her down crowded halls, jerking her to halts that nearly unseated her, and scraping her through doorways. He had blamed her for

10

not trying hard enough when it became evident his drills and exercises were not going to put her miraculously back on her feet like a heroine in some inspirational drama. As if she would still be sitting in this chair or any other if sheer determination could set her free.

"Is it fun to ride like that?" Pam asked.

Kirsty turned to stare at her. "What do you think?"

"I think it's neat. You've got a lot of neat stuff." Pam shut the desk drawer she was opening and directed a grin at the door. "Right, Daddy?"

Gene Hamilton, Kirsty's father, stood smiling in the doorway. "I see you've been doing some serious unpacking. That's a good way to get acquainted."

"I was done before she came in," Kirsty said. She wished he would give Pam the lecture he had so often repeated to her and Gail about respecting other people's property. This Pam kid had obviously never heard it.

"Look. She's all moved in." A sweep of Pam's arm indicated the entire room.

Gene Hamilton nodded, his gaze taking in details one by one. Kirsty watched for his reaction to the silver-framed photograph, but there was none. His eyes moved on to the empty suitcase on the bed. "If you're done with that, I'll take it out of here. Everything okay?"

It was Kirsty's turn to nod. "I guess—" Nothing was okay, really, of course. This was not the kind of house they used to live in, she and her family. This was not the family they used to have. This was not the way they used to talk, she and her father—politely, like strangers not

11

quite comfortable with each other. And they never used to have their privacy intruded on by third parties who actually were strangers but didn't seem to know it.

Pam tugged at his free hand as he lifted the suitcase. "When are we going to start the fire?"

"As a matter of fact, I was cruising just now for volunteers to help carry in wood. Snow is starting to come down in buckets out there, so we better get at it."

The cat Toby emerged from under the bed and trotted after them out of the room. Kirsty was left staring at an empty door. Not a parting glance or nod for her from any of them.

The tiny ache prodded again behind her eyes. If anyone in this house was a stranger and out of place, it was she.

2

THE LIVING ROOM was a place of lights and shadows when Kirsty wheeled herself in through the arched door-way an hour later. Birch logs were blazing in the stone fireplace at the farther end of the room, the flames reflected in a row of long, tall front windows.

No one had looked in on her during that hour to see how she was doing, and no one had invited her to be a part of the action she could hear going on in various parts of the house—doors banging open and shut, feet tramping out and in, spurts of laughter and conversation.

She was tempted to respond with a cool, "No, thank you. I'm not hungry," when Rita called, "Kirsty, are you ready for a picnic? We're in the living room." But she was hungry, and Pam's shrill "I'll go get her" got her instantly moving out under her own power.

Her chair rolled smoothly over the flat hall carpeting.

It took more effort to push on across the plush on the living room floor, but she made it without anyone's help to the edge of a plastic shower curtain spread like a picnic blanket in front of the hearth.

"See, I told you we're having a wienie roast," Pam beamed, skipping alongside her.

Rita was bent above a tea cart laden with hot dogs and buns, potato chips, paper plates, and assorted jars and relish pots. Her smile was brightly cordial as if she were welcoming a visitor. "We like indoor picnics, especially when the weather is doing its worst outside."

Kirsty's father was arranging fat, lawn-chair type cushions on the shower curtain like seats at a campfire.

"Kirsty should have the striped one," Pam decreed. "That's the newest and she's the newest, too."

"Unless you'd be more comfortable in your chair, Kirsty," Rita added. She was doing the correct, considerate hostess role to perfection.

Kirsty set her brake and shifted her footrest down out of the way. "I'll sit on the floor. I'll sit next to my dad."

Her father helped her slip down onto the red-striped cushion. "We're doing a replay of our first supper here, since you missed that one. Except that evening we ate in here because the power was off and the stove wouldn't work. We had to rough it or starve."

Pam plopped herself on the cushion on Kirsty's other side. "We couldn't even go out to McDonald's. Remember? Because it was storming so hard and lightning. A

14

power line came down right across the driveway, and shot up humongous blue sparks."

"Don't remind me." Rita handed her and Kirsty each a long, slender stick with a skewered wiener on the end. "I thought this house was going to end up in Oz before that storm was over. And it had started by being such a beautiful day for moving."

"Lucky for us we had this fireplace and there was some old wood in the garage," Pam said, thrusting her stick into the center of the flames.

"I wouldn't say luck had too much to do with it," Kirsty's father said as he folded himself on the cushion next to Kirsty. "Your mother told the realtor she didn't want to look at any house without a fireplace. My guess is the idea of a living room cookout crossed her mind the first time she set foot in this place."

Kirsty was startled by his chuckle, by the fondness in it.

Rita chuckled, too, seated on the cushion opposite him. It didn't seem to trouble her that Kirsty had the spot closest to him. "My whole life I've dreamed of putting down roots somewhere. You can't put down roots living in apartments. It takes a real house, and a real house should have a fireplace—among other things."

She and Kirsty's father looked at each other and smiled—looks and smiles that scraped across Kirsty's heart like sandpaper. How could they be so cozy together? How could he betray his real wife, Kirsty's mother, like this?

Who was this Rita person, anyway? Definitely she was not pretty like Kirsty's mother. Not downright homely like Pam, but the family resemblance was there. She could also stand to lose a couple of pounds, a fact her stained white sweatshirt, stamped UNIVERSITY OF WISCONSIN across the chest, was not designed to hide.

Kirsty's mother had been so trim and dainty always, even in grubby garden jeans and her hair windblown—hair the color of sunshine.

Rita's hair was an unremarkable rusty brown. At that, it was her best feature, especially when the fire glow struck red highlights from it. Possibly that was another reason she had insisted on a house where she could sit by a fire.

Kirsty fixed her eyes on the wiener roasting at the end of her stick. She knew she should look up in acknowledgment when Rita passed her a plate piled with chips and pickles and a bun, but she couldn't do it. She couldn't bear just yet to give the woman that much recognition.

"Don't you say thank you anymore?" her father asked. He had stopped smiling.

Kirsty felt the heat of the fire flare in her face. At the same time, she felt as if she were carved in ice. "Thank you," she muttered to the plate.

Rita became occupied distributing the other plates. Cheery as a Scout leader, she said, "The buns are already buttered. Beyond that, everybody's on their own."

"Yum. Super hot dogs." Pam removed hers from its

stick and proceeded to layer mustard, relish, and catsup into its bun. "Super delicious."

Kirsty's, similarly treated, tasted like wood in her mouth. She chewed and swallowed, and swallowed again. It helped some when her father handed her a can of Sprite to wash it down, but only some.

Her mother would have served milk or apple juice with a meal like this, and carrot sticks or a salad.

Her mother would not have approved of how Pam was cramming in potato chips by the handful.

Her mother would have seen how badly Kirsty was aching inside. And her mother would have cared.

Kirsty turned her face away from the fire. Her reflection, a pale-faced girl in a yellow turtleneck, glimmered at her from the nearest of the four tall windows. A mirror image of the firelit room floated there, hovering floorless against the faint sheen of snow at night.

Strange how different everything looked just by being in reverse. Details she had barely noted in the real room fairly jumped at her from the glass—like the balding spot on the back of her father's head; the ever-present darkness behind the dancing flames; the panels of the shadowy door on the other side of the room . . .

Kirsty frowned. She hadn't noticed that door before. How could she have missed it?

She twisted to scan the real room again. A russet couch between two end tables and two lighted lamps occupied the space. Nothing else.

She turned back to the window. There were the lamps and the couch, sharp and clear. No door. No shadows. And no longer the illusion that the room was lit mainly by firelight.

"Something the matter, Kirsty?" her father asked. "Are you getting tired?"

"No, I'm fine." She gulped down the last of her Sprite to prove it.

These were old windows, antiques practically, and the glass tended to distort things sometimes. Rita herself had told her so this afternoon while giving her a first-floor tour of the house. No need to make an issue of the fact the light was playing tricks.

"I know what you're doing." Pam leaned to peer past her. "You can see us in the window. So can I."

"Yes, I see," Rita said. "Look at us there, all neatly framed." She laughed. "Our first family portrait. *Family by the Fire*, we should call it."

Kirsty flinched. How could the woman even pretend they were anything like a family? As for the fire—"Witch's fire," Kirsty said before she could stop herself.

Pam's eyes widened at her. "What?"

"Witch's fire," Kirsty repeated, a touch defiantly. "That's what it's called when you can see the fire in the window and it looks like it's outdoors and backward. My sister told me. She read it in a book."

She was careful not to look at her father. He hated anything that smacked of superstition. The one truly

18

heated quarrel she could recall witnessing between her parents had to do with her mother's telling her and Gail of the Pollard family tradition that every other generation or so produced someone able to sense or hear or see things beyond the ken of everyday mortals. Kirsty and Gail had secretly practiced seeing, hearing, and sensing for several days afterward until it became all too evident that either they were not among the gifted or that their father's verdict of "unmitigated nonsense" was right.

"Witch's fire," Pam echoed in a hushed voice. "And this is a witch's house."

Gene Hamilton tapped her on the shoulder. "I beg your pardon, ma'am, but I thought we had that all straightened out. This is *our* house. Before that, it belonged to a Miss Potter, who was the kindergarten teacher at Frederiksen Elementary, and I have yet to hear of any kindergartner that got turned into a toad."

Pam ducked her head and giggled, but her grin lacked conviction. "Frederiksen Elementary, that's my school. The kindergarten teachers are Miss Nolan and Mrs. Michaels."

"Miss Potter—Alma, I think her name is—is an old, old lady at Custer Memorial Manor," Rita said. "She must be very frail. They've never brought her down for any therapy that I know of. I don't believe I've ever seen her."

A warning light flickered in Kirsty's brain. "What is Custer Memorial Manor?"

Rita smiled. "It's the nursing home where I work."

19

"My mom's a physical therapist," Pam supplied, as if it were information worthy of trumpets. "Do you know what that is?"

"Yes, I know what that is," Kirsty snapped. Was she likely to forget her knowledge of nursing home therapists and their power to inflict humiliations and pain? "But I didn't know that she was one." She glared at her father. "You never told me."

"I told you," her father said. "I know I told you. When I first told you about Rita—"

Kirsty shook her head. "You said she worked. You didn't say where. You didn't say—"

Her voice broke. If only she could jump up and flounce furiously from the room. But that was the point, wasn't it? She couldn't.

Was that how Rita had snared him into marriage? Had she told him on the hope that having a live-in therapist on hand twenty-four hours a day might mean he wouldn't be saddled with a kid in a wheelchair the rest of his life?

"Custer Manor is a really neat place," Pam said. "Specially the part where my mom works. There's a swimming pool and a whirlpool and different tables you can lie on and get jiggled. It's fun."

"No thanks," Kirsty said. "I've seen all the nursing homes I ever care to."

"We should take her over there some day, right, Mom?" said Pam, who apparently had a problem understanding plain English. "We could swim and stuff, couldn't we?"

"We could," Rita nodded, "if the time ever comes that

Kirsty feels she might like to. Let's leave it up to her."

Kirsty slid her finger around the edge of her plate, driving stray potato chip crumbs into a drift. Didn't anybody this far north understand *No?*

The wooden hot dog she had eaten was bumping against the walls of her stomach, wanting out. Her father was breaking the burning logs apart with the poker.

An orange paw suddenly snaked up over the rim of her plate. It slapped lightly at her finger and disappeared.

Kirsty screamed. It wasn't that she was hurt. The slap might have been a tap from a powder puff. Neither was she genuinely frightened. She had seen the cat tiptoeing along the edge of the spread-out shower curtain, sniffing inquiringly at the plastic.

It was just that a scream had been lurking in her throat, so close to the surface that any jolt would have let it go.

Pam's stare was a mixture of pity and disgust. "Toby thought you wanted to play with him, wiggling your finger like that. He wasn't going to bite."

"He surprised me. That's all." Kirsty had about had her fill of surprises for one evening.

"I don't think Kirsty's been around pets much. She's not used to them," her father said. He made it sound like an apology for her, not a defense. He could have added that the lack of pets was not from choice but because his other daughter, Gail, had been allergic to fur. But he didn't.

Pam pulled the cat into her lap and rubbed her cheek against the top of his head. "Toby's not a pet. He's a fur

21

person. He's my best friend. When he sleeps with me at night, I don't get nightmares." She raised her chin. "And he doesn't makes smells in the closet, does he, Mom?"

"Well, he did in mine," Kirsty retorted. "It was so bad that even he was sneezing. And it made my head ache."

Rita stretched a hand to stroke the cat. "I'm sure it wasn't Toby's doing. I just don't understand what it could have been. What sort of smell was it?"

Kirsty wrinkled her nose. How did a person describe a smell? "Like garbage burning. Kind of. Rotten, smelly, stale smoke. I don't know. I never smelled anything like it."

Her father's face was unbelieving. "That room's just been redone from floor to ceiling—painted, papered, carpeted. There can't be anything in there that smells like that."

"Gene, wait." Rita sat forward on her cushion. "What about that old stove in the basement? You were burning trash in it yesterday. It's just about under that room, isn't it?"

"There's nothing wrong with that stove," Gene Hamilton said in a tone that suggested he had said this before. "I've had it checked."

"I know, but still— Maybe I'm a nut about carbon monoxide and such, but if fumes are seeping up from somewhere—"

"Carbon monoxide doesn't smell, and there aren't any fumes of any kind seeping up from that stove. I made sure everything was out before I left it yesterday." He reached for a handful of potato chips and began munching as though the subject were closed.

"All the same," Rita said, ignoring the signal, "it's not impossible something might have been smoldering and flared up again later." She was gathering her legs under her.

"Rita, I just told you—"

"It won't hurt for me to run down and have a quick look. To be absolutely on the safe side."

"I'll go, too." Pam released Toby and jumped up.

"Rita—"

Kirsty recognized that thin edge of irritation in her father's voice, but Rita and Pam were on their way out the door. He pitched his wadded paper napkin into the fire and stood up to follow.

"Daddy?" Kirsty's chair was beyond her reach, and she didn't want to be left stranded on the floor.

He turned in the doorway, frowning, then strode back to lift her with more haste than ceremony. "Sorry, puss. We won't be long."

She watched him tramp off down the hall in pursuit of the others. He was really annoyed. And not at her. At his wonderful Rita, who didn't seem quite so wonderful to him when she wouldn't listen.

The price of triumph, though, was that Kirsty was once more left behind, the outsider in someone else's house.

She rolled her chair away from the picnic litter on the floor, telling herself that this time she didn't care that much.

A log collapsed in the fireplace. A blaze of sparks shot upward. Reflected fire flashed from the fourth window like a beacon, drawing her eyes to the glass.

And there again was that shadowy door. Yet not quite so shadowy as before. And no longer tightly shut. It now stood slightly ajar, offering a glimpse into the room beyond. A glimpse of—what?

Kirsty inched closer, only half-believing. She expected any moment the image would waver and split into slivers of unfocused light, or be blotted out by her own approaching shadow.

Instead, it held steady, growing clearer if anything, the nearer she came.

A hiss exploded at her feet, and Toby hurtled onto a footstool just below the sill. He glared through the pane, his tail bushed, his ears flattened as they had been when he burst from her closet.

That same instant, the window went blank. Kirsty and the cat were gazing into darkness.

She blinked, and tears stung in her eyes as if she were a little girl who had lost a piece of candy.

Except the loss was more than candy. What she had glimpsed beyond that partly open door—what she was almost sure she had glimpsed—was the corner of a couch. A flowered couch the same as the one in the photograph beside her bed.

3

KIRSTY STOPPED in the living room after breakfast the next morning. Half a dozen times during the night she had told herself that what she had seen was her imagination, tricked by the firelight on a bulge in the glass. That had to be it.

Yet it was something of a letdown to find the four tall windows looking exactly as she had expected—as ordinary and unremarkable as four windows could be. There was nothing to see but a whitened front yard studded with dark, snow-streaked evergreens whose drooping branches all but hid the existence of a street beyond them. It might have been a Christmas card scene, except that it inspired her with no sense of glad tidings or good cheer.

She was tired and achy this morning, and Rita had not improved matters by asking at breakfast if she had any exercises to keep her muscles toned. Kirsty did, in fact, but they could not make her able to walk again and she didn't always bother to do them. Already Rita was moving in on her—and with her father's full approval, to judge by the solicitous way he had leaned over Rita to pour her a second cup of coffee. His irritation of the evening had evaporated somewhere in the night.

Kirsty couldn't resist wheeling across the room to examine the window that had done such odd reflecting by firelight. There was a crank in the sill that turned easily under an experimental twist of her hand, but turn was all it did. Nothing else happened.

"Hi. What are you trying to do?" Pam said behind her. "Let Toby out?"

Kirsty jumped as if she had been caught spying on secrets. "Toby? What do you mean?"

"Toby." Pam tugged at her sagging pajama bottoms and pointed to where the cat sat under an end table, regarding them through sleepy eyes. "He likes to go in and out these windows. Only not that one."

"Why not? What's wrong with it?" Kirsty wiggled the crank again, rather pleased that this window really was a little different from the others.

"I don't know. It's stuck or broken. Daddy's going to fix it some day when he gets time. But the rest are okay." Pam grasped the crank on the next sill. "Watch."

The window swung slowly outward from top to bottom, letting in a shaft of frosty air.

"See? They're like doors, kind of. Except it's a pretty far step down on the other side."

Toby at once sprang onto the sill. He stood, tail tip flicking to and fro, considering the snowy landscape.

Kirsty shivered, feeling the chill in every drop of her Florida-thinned blood. "Okay. Okay. Now shut it."

Pam's monkey face registered surprise. "Are you cold?" She ruffled the fur along Toby's back. "Come on, Toby. Make up your mind. In or out?"

Toby chose out. He launched himself lightly into space and dropped from Kirsty's line of vision.

"Now shut it," she insisted.

Instead, Pam thrust her head out past the window frame and giggled. "Toby doesn't like the snow. Look at him lift his feet and shake them."

"The window," Kirsty reminded her. "Close it." But she was curious enough to lean closer to her own window to see what the cat was doing.

The effort was wasted. Her window had grown a coat of fog impossible to see through.

Pam pulled her head in and began winding the window shut. "There he goes, but look, he's still shaking his feet. Isn't he funny?"

Kirsty swept her sleeve across the foggy pane to clear it. All she accomplished was to create a grimy smear that was worse than the fog. She couldn't make out even the shadow of a cat through it.

"Oh, hey, what's that?" With her window shut, Pam's interest returned to Kirsty's. "What are you doing?"

"Trying to get this window clean," Kirsty said irritably. She pitied the patients at the nursing home if Rita were no better at therapy than she was at housekeeping.

"No, wait. It's like a face." Pam's finger became a pointer again. "There's the nose, and the eyes, and that's the chin."

Kirsty stopped her arm on the brink of another sweep. The smear did resemble a hazy sort of face, the more so the more she stared at it. An old, gray face slyly staring back at her.

Pam's finger swooped to draw a broad U under the jagged slant of the nose. "And there's a happy smile."

Happy smile, indeed. All at once the blur on the glass was leering at them as if it had just seen what it was going to have for lunch.

"Gross," Kirsty declared, and leaned to scrub her arm hard across the ugly thing.

"Yuk!" Pam leaped backward with an exaggerated squeal, at the same time giving a yank to Kirsty's chair. "It's the witch! Get away!"

Kirsty was caught off-balance. She pitched forward as the solid surface of the window receded beyond her bent arm. Her grab at the arms overbalanced the chair as well. It began to tip along with her. For a crazy instant she felt as if a force stronger than gravity were pulling her. The gray smear on the window looked like an opening she was about to plunge straight through.

Her scream and Pam's shrilled together. Kirsty was almost glad of the resounding thud when her head struck the very solid glass a fraction before her outflung hands did.

"I'm sorry. I'm sorry," Pam was wailing, her hands clamped on the chair back to drag it upright.

Kirsty squared herself on the seat and pressed fingers to her temple, waiting for a wash of dizziness to pass. In a voice so tight it was barely a whisper, she said, "Don't you ever do that again. Don't you ever touch my chair again—ever, Ever, EVER."

"Girls?" Rita called from the kitchen. "Where are you? What's going on?"

Kirsty's father came running down the stairs. "Kirsty? Pam? What's the matter? Somebody get hurt?"

Pam hurled herself into his arms. "It was an accident. I didn't mean to."

"Okay, okay," he said. "Calm down. Tell me what happened."

Kirsty's voice regained its power. "She tried to dump me on the floor."

"Pam!" Rita said from the doorway. "You didn't."

"I was just playing," Pam wept against Kirsty's father. "I didn't know she would tip."

"She jerked the chair and I hit my head against the window," Kirsty charged.

Tears were brimming in her eyes, too, much as she hated to look like a baby.

"Dumping people on the floor isn't my idea of play-ing," Rita said severely. "I'm surprised at you, Pam. Let me see, Kirsty."

29

Kirsty turned her head so her father could see the bruise, too. It was his sympathy she wanted, not Rita's. Why was Rita being such a bundle of concern about her while he stood there consoling Pam as if she were the injured party? Were he and Rita trying to make points with each other, each sticking up for the other one's kid?

Kirsty glared at Pam. "She wasn't playing. She thought a patch of steam on the window was a witch face looking in. She's got witches on the brain."

"It could have been a witch. You don't know," Pam retorted, lifting her face to wipe a sleeve across her wet freckles. "It could have been a witch that made you tip, not me. Maybe she wanted to snatch you out through the window."

Kirsty's skin prickled. That was too close to her own stupid fantasy to be amusing.

"If there is a witch, you're the one she's probably after," she countered. "Witches always go for little kids. Maybe she's hanging around for a chance to grab you out of bed some night and gobble you up."

"Witches don't gobble you up," Pam said with scorn. "They put spells on you so you have accidents or get sick and die. Only they have to start with like a piece of your fingernail or your hair." She clasped her hands quickly behind her. "But nobody can get my fingernails because I bite them off and chew them up."

"All right," Kirsty's father cut in. "Let's put a lid on this witch business right now. I told you last night I don't want to hear any more about witches in this house, and

I meant it. I don't care if you were just playing or what. *No more witches.*" He gave Pam a little shake. "Understood?"

Pam nodded, giggling. She wasn't the least bit scared by him. And Kirsty could tell he wasn't seriously annoyed with Pam, not for insisting on witches, not for hurting his own child.

She scowled at the window. The fog patch had thinned away to nothing by itself. Any spying witch that might have been must have gone off well satisfied with the mischief she had caused.

"Let me get you a piece of ice for that bump, Kirsty," Rita said.

"Let me. I'll get it." Pam was off and running. "I'll get you a whole bowlful."

"No, never mind. It's okay," Kirsty called after her. Must this kid turn everything into a circus? "It doesn't hurt that bad."

"I think what would do you both good is a dose of fresh air and sunshine," her father said. "Maybe Pam can give you a tour of the neighborhood. The sun looks like it's coming out, so the snow should be gone off the walks in a little while."

Pam's pajama-clad figure changed course in mid-gallop. "Super. I'll go get my clothes on."

Kirsty cringed. Another hour or two of Pam's company this morning was asking too much.

"I can't. It's so cold out there. I don't have any winter clothes."

That was no lie. Her winter coat and jackets of two years ago hadn't even gone with her to Florida, and they would be outgrown now if they had.

"Let's see if I can't find something that will do," Rita said in a no-problem voice. "We can always pad you out in layers even if there's not a perfect fit."

She disappeared up the stairs behind Pam.

Kirsty had an inspiration. "Daddy, why don't you show me the neighborhood? Couldn't we go out by ourselves? Just you and me, I mean. Together?"

She wouldn't mind the cold if he said yes. They hadn't been alone together since she arrived. Nor for a long time before that.

"Leave Pam behind, you mean?" He shook his head. "I doubt that's humanly possible. She's so glad to have you here, she can hardly stand it. You ought to be flattered."

He chuckled, but Kirsty didn't smile.

"Why me? I don't even know her. Doesn't she have any friends her own size?"

Again he shook his head. "She's almost as new to these parts as you are. Also, for some reason, there aren't many children living close by here. Poor little kid, we're about all the people she's got."

And how many people did he think Kirsty had? Why couldn't she make him hear what she was saying? "Can't you come along? I don't want to go unless you go."

"I don't want to spoil her fun," he said, still not hearing. "Kids don't want grownups tagging along when they're

32

out exploring. I tell you what: you and Pam do the neighborhood this morning, and maybe after lunch we'll all pile into the car and take the grand tour of Frederiksen. How about that?"

All of them? The bump on her temple really was beginning to throb. "Sure. Super," she said, giving up.

If she collapsed of pain halfway down the street or returned from the expedition dying of pneumonia, no doubt they would all attend the funeral together, too. Unless, of course, that might spoil some fun for Pam.

She went back to her room yearning to throw something. A drawing pad lay on her desk. She snatched up a dark crayon and slashed a few swift, angry strokes across the paper.

In less than a minute the witch image from the window was smirking up at her in shadings of charcoal gray. Kirsty added a scrawny neck beneath the chin, a more defined squint to the eyes, a beaklike lift to the nose. The gray face sharpened, grew craftier, and gratifyingly more menacing.

She stood the sketch against the desk lamp to study it. What a pity she couldn't creep upstairs and tack the thing to Pam's bedroom door.

She sat a minute, imagining hauling herself up step by step by means of the stair rail. It would take forever, and was certainly nothing she could hope to manage in secret.

Strange to remember how once she used to sprint up a flight of stairs without giving the effort a second thought. She used to do gymnastics just as easily—better

33

even than Gail. That had been the one accomplishment of her life that had made her father truly proud.

The witch face leered at her knowingly. Kirsty suddenly had seen as much of it as she wanted. She tore the sheet from the pad, meaning to rip it up. The paper refused to tear that readily, and she had no patience for shredding it bit by bit.

No time, either, for she could hear Pam and Rita descending the stairs. She yanked the desk drawer open, stuffed the sketch in facedown, plopped the drawing pad in on top of it, and slammed the drawer shut.

4

A PALE YELLOW sun shone in a pale blue sky as Kirsty eased down the ramp her father had built over the steps from the kitchen door to the driveway. The radio in the kitchen was still exclaiming over the freak storm that had hit Frederiksen late yesterday, dumping up to four inches of snow on the north side of town while barely dusting the south. Kirsty didn't have to be told that this was the north side.

True to her father's prediction, most of the snow that had fallen on pavement had thawed away. The brown lawns and rusty weed patches she had seen on her arrival yesterday, however, lay now buried under one broad and boldly contoured sweep of white.

True to Kirsty's prediction, there was a biting chill to the air. A cutting edge of wind found her through the bulky sweatshirt parka and oversized wool pants she wore.

Pam jogged happily beside her down the drive. She waved at the house when they turned onto the sidewalk in front of it. "Hi, Toby," she called.

Through a gap in the pines, Kirsty caught a glimpse of red brick walls and creamy white trim. The cat, a splash of orange draped across the back of a chair, was watching them from one of the tall living room windows.

"You know what?" Pam asked. "He never tries to come in or go out that one window that won't open. It's like he knows it's bad. He's so smart."

His smartness went beyond that, Kirsty reflected, shivering. He had long since returned from his tour of this winter wonderland and was cozily settled indoors for the rest of the day.

She did a zigzag to pull ahead of Pam and speed up their pace. "Let's make this as fast as we can."

Pam gave a yip of consent and broke into a run.

Theirs was the only house at this upper end of a sloping street. They sped the length of the block to round the corner onto a side street where half a dozen uniform frame houses sat looking as if they had resolutely turned their backs to the brick one.

Two bikes glided across the farther end of this street, a red bike and a blue one. Kirsty once had owned a blue ten-speed. Gail's had been red. Kirsty might have preferred red, but Gail, being two years older, got hers first and, of course, had first pick of colors.

Pam gazed after the bikes as they passed from sight. She slowed to a walk, then did an abrupt about-face. "Let's not go this way. Let's go back around the other way."

Kirsty slowed, too, partly because there was less of a slope to carry her along in this direction. The brick house, she saw now, stood on the crest of a rise, considerably above any of its neighbors.

"No way," she said, thinking of the uphill pull. "Come on."

Pam came to a halt, hesitating, but Kirsty moved briskly on. Reluctantly, Pam shuffled into a trot to catch up.

The houses did not invite lingering, even though they did offer some protection from the wind. There was a closed quality about them as if they had gone into hibernation with the snow.

The only house on the third side of the block was painted an apple green that was meant, no doubt, to be cheerful. To Kirsty it looked all the more forlorn under the snow mounded on its eaves and over its door. Or perhaps it was Kirsty who was forlornly noting as she turned the corner that she was now halfway around the block and had as far left to go as she had already come.

"Hey, Peanut!" A shout from behind Pam and her broke the stillness.

"Who's that?" Kirsty asked.

"Nobody." Pam cast a wary look backward and quickened her steps. "Come on. Let's go really fast.

"Pea-nut!" The red bike flashed by them, swung in a tight circle, and darted into the driveway of the green house just ahead of them. It braked crosswise of the walk, barring the way.

The blue bike skidded to a stop at the curb.

"Where you think you're going, Peanut?" the boy on the red bike demanded. He was about Kirsty's age, a thin-faced boy in a torn gray sweater and no cap on his straight black hair.

Pam hunched deeper inside her jacket. "Around the block."

The boy eyed Kirsty, then spoke past her again to Pam. "Who's this? This the new sister you been talking about?"

Kirsty resented being treated like a piece of furniture incapable of speaking for herself. "I'm not her sister and she's not mine. Her name is Gunther. Mine's Hamilton."

The boy granted her a blink of attention and a shrug.

"Her name is Peanut," the boy on the blue bike said, snickering. He was a replica of the other boy except for being a year or two younger and dressed in an unzipped nylon jacket.

"Yeah, Peanut. Short for Peanut Face." The first boy screwed his own face into what he apparently considered a comic imitation of Pam's and thrust it toward them. "Right, Peanut?"

Pam shrank from him but produced a small, sickly grin.

"Who are you supposed to be?" Kirsty challenged. She stared at him as if she were deliberately memorizing his raw, chapped face adorned by a nose that jutted like a cup handle. "I know it's not Mr. America."

The comedian bugged his eyes at her. "Just call me Alf. You know, A-L-F, like for Alien Life Form."

"He's Alf Thayer," Pam supplied in a near-whisper. "And that's Dean. The one I told you that says we live in a witch's house."

Alf shifted his bug-eyed gaze to her. "You think he's kidding? Hey, you ask our cousin, Lisa. Old Lady Potter almost got her. Said she wanted Lisa to help her house-clean, but what she really wanted was to zap her. That's what she's lived on all these years, the life power she zaps out of other people, mostly girls."

"Yeah," Dean said. "Mostly girls. But Lisa knew what to look out for. She smelled the old lady cooking up a mess of stink in the basement, so she locked the door on her and took off. Otherwise, nobody might ever have seen her again."

"That's how come you're living in that house," Alf added. "Old Lady Potter missed her fix last time, and turned so old they had to take her away to the nursing home."

"You said she tried to burn the house down," Pam charged. "That's what you said the witch did."

"She did." Dean tugged at his jacket, which apparently had a broken zipper. "The power lines came down across the roof and the wiring inside started a fire in the walls the day the For Sale sign went up. It rained and blew so

39

hard the fire department could hardly get there. I know because our dad's a fireman."

Kirsty studied the boys' solemn faces, searching for the grin that had to be lurking somewhere.

"Listen," Alf said, still solemn. "She tried the same thing the day your folks moved in, except you were lucky. That time the lines missed the house."

Kirsty was annoyed at herself for visibly shivering. Now they would think they had succeeded in scaring her, when in fact she was simply freezing to death just sitting here. She could feel her blood icing to slush. "Sounds like the poor old dear is losing her touch," she said, looking past the red bike to the stretch of clear sidewalk beyond.

Dean rubbed his nose on the knit cuff of his sleeve. "She ain't dead yet. And she don't want nobody living in that house but her."

"Unless maybe two nice, fresh, juicy girls," Alf said, and now he did grin.

Dean nodded. "My dad says he wouldn't set foot in that place for a million after taxes. Who knows what old magic or spells could still be hanging around?"

Alf crimped his wheel and rolled his bike more directly toward them. "Don't say nobody warned you." He jerked a thumb at the wheelchair. "You won't get far taking off at the last minute in that thing."

Kirsty was eyeing the space his move had opened up in front of her. "Watch me."

She pulled out, around, and past him before he could

shift to stop her. Pam was quick to catch up to her and take the lead. "Your daddy's dumb," she yelled at Dean. "We don't even talk about witches at our house, because we know there is no such thing."

"Oh, yeah?" Dean yelled back. "You're the one that's dumb. You'll find out, Peanut Face."

His bike darted by them to where snow lay drifted beneath a roadside tree farther on. Jumping off, he scooped together a hasty handful of snow and flung it at Pam.

It missed her by the width of the sidewalk to land in a wet splatter in Kirsty's lap. She swept up the fragments, packed them solid, and lobbed the missile back where it came from.

It was a long time since she had thrown a ball of any sort, but the swing of her arm felt right.

An explosion of slush blossomed on the front of Dean's jacket.

"Ha, ha, Dean," Pam jeered. "You're the one that's dumb."

Dean sent a second snowball flying past them.

"Ha, ha, missed again." Pam dodged behind Kirsty's chair and popped up on the other side with another fistful of snow for her. "Here. Hit him again."

"She won't come close," Alf called, circling by to join Dean. "That was just a lucky shot."

Kirsty's second ball smashed against his shoulder as he threw himself from his bike. His black brows arched up as if he hadn't quite seen her before. Then he was crouched behind the tree, scraping up ammunition of his own.

Kirsty realized she was grinning as snowballs began sailing to and fro in earnest, although the boys had the advantage. Alf's aim was better than Dean's, and the girls had no tree to hide behind. Nor could Kirsty reach the snow beside the walk without the risk of overbalancing herself.

"Hurry up. Give me some more," she kept urging Pam.

Pam was no less busy collecting handfuls to hurl herself. She was dancing here and there like an excited puppy, sometimes right into the line of fire.

One snowball struck her full in the mouth. She rubbed her chin, and stood suddenly motionless while another snowball broke against her shoulder and a third whitened the tassel of her knit cap.

"Duck, dummy," Kirsty shrieked at her. She yanked at Pam's sleeve as Alf's head appeared around the tree trunk, lining up his next shot. "Get down. Get down."

Pam sank onto her heels and pulled off her mitten. "My tooth got knocked out," she said, poking a finger in her mouth. "My loose tooth."

"Ya, ya, Peanut Face," Dean yelled. "Giving up? Got enough? Want—"

His voice was drowned by the blast of a car horn. A white minivan cruised to a halt just short of where the two bikes lay against the curb, and an angry voice shouted, "Shame on you boys. What do you think you're doing? You ought to be reported."

Alf and Dean were already on their bikes and streaking off down the street. The minivan blatted a parting trio of toots to hasten them on their way.

"You girls stay where you are," a gray-haired woman in a fuzzy lavender hat directed from the driver's window.

The minivan swung left into the next driveway, where the garage opened automatically to receive it.

Alf was right about one thing, Kirsty had to concede. She wasn't equipped for a fast getaway like his and Dean's.

Besides that, Pam was down on all fours on the sidewalk.

"What are you doing now?" Kirsty asked in exasperation.

"My tooth. Don't move. I dropped my tooth, and I have to find it for under my pillow."

Kirsty groaned. "Get real. Now it's going to be the Tooth Fairy? Come on."

"I am real," Pam said, scrabbling among clods of snow. "Last summer I got one dollar for a tooth, and this one's bigger."

The woman in the lavender hat rushed from the garage to bend over her. "Oh, sweetie, did you fall down?"

"She lost a baby tooth," Kirsty said, hoping to head off another melodrama like Pam's performance in the living room this morning. "A loose one. We're okay."

"I found it." Pam bobbed up triumphantly. "See?" She held out her palm, the tooth nestled in its hollow. "I didn't like to wiggle it too much because it hurt, kind of, but now it's out, and I'm going to be rich."

"Well—" The indignant pink of the woman's face began to fade. "They say it's an ill wind that blows nobody good. And that Thayer tribe is about as ill a wind as anybody could wish for, always in trouble or causing some. There was a time I hoped for better from these two. Their father does try."

Pam was not one to pass up an offer of sympathy. "They keep saying we live in a witch's house. Our daddy doesn't like that."

The woman gave them a sharpened glance. "You're the little girl in the Potter house, aren't you? I thought I'd seen you. And you have to be—" She rested a lavender-gloved hand on Kirsty's shoulder. "Let me think. I saw your name in our files yesterday. Krissy, isn't it?"

"Kirsty," Kirsty said, and received an approving pat for being right.

"Kirsty. Yes. And I'm Mrs. Vohl. I work in the office at the Middle School." Another pat. "I think you'll like our school. We're all ready for you to start Monday."

Kirsty stared up at her. "Monday? *This* Monday?"

A long while ago her father had mentioned that she would likely have to attend regular school when she came here rather than go on studying at home as she was with Grandma Pollard. He hadn't said she would have to face that hurdle the minute she arrived here, though. She had thought maybe at the start of the new semester, after

Christmas. At least not until after Thanksgiving. Monday was day after tomorrow.

"That's the word we have," Mrs. Vohl said as if she were delivering a winning lottery ticket. "The paper work is all done, the school bus driver has a seat reserved for you, and everything is set to go."

Except me, Kirsty thought. Her hands clenched themselves inside her mittens. When had they planned to let her in on the surprise, her father and Rita? Monday morning when the bus pulled up?

"We're not in the Potter house," Pam corrected Mrs. Vohl. "We're in the Hamilton house. My daddy is Gene Hamilton, and he bought it."

"Of course," Mrs. Vohl agreed. "It's just that Alma Potter lived there so many years—since it was built, I think. Long before I was born, if you can imagine that. Since before my mother's time, too. I don't doubt she'd be there still if she hadn't fallen in her cellar and broken her hip, poor thing. When someone finally found her, she was too near gone to object to anything."

Pam was gazing at Mrs. Vohl in awe. "Were you friends with her?"

"Well—" Mrs. Vohl considered. " 'Acquainted' might be a better term. There's such a difference in our ages. Although she did use to take in some young person or other from time to time, girls mostly. She said they kept her young, and it must have been so, for she hardly looked a day over forty right up until she had her accident."

45

"And then what?" Pam asked.

"Well, then it was like she aged a hundred years over-night." Mrs. Vohl shook her head. "Strange. So strange. And terrible. She'd been lying helpless in that cellar no one knows how long."

The wind was flattening Kirsty's sweatshirt against her chest and slipping frosty fingers inside her hood. She didn't want to sit here chatting. She wanted to get back to the house where it was warm and where she could find out more about this school-on-Monday business. Yet she couldn't keep from asking, "What became of all those girls?"

"Oh, I don't know," Mrs. Vohl said airily. "They were strays pretty much, in trouble with the law or their folks or drugs. That kind is hard to track when they decide to drift on to somewhere else or plain disappear. None of them lasted here very long, I know."

This time it was more than the wind that caused Kirsty to shiver. "Come on," she told Pam. "We have to get home."

"My tooth," Pam cried, and dove to the rescue as it slid through her fingers again.

"You're going to be bankrupt before you get home," Mrs. Vohl said, laughing. "Here, wait a minute."

She opened her handbag, black leather with lavender trim, and produced a key ring from which dangled a flat pumpkin shape of bright orange. "I won this at a Hal-loween party, and have been wondering what to do with is ever since. See, it's a little purse. Put your tooth in there and if you drop it, you'll have no trouble spotting where it went."

Pam blossomed into one wide, delighted smile. "Thank you. That's perfect. Orange is my favorite color, too. I even have an orange cat. His name is Toby."

"A cat? A real cat?" Mrs. Vohl repeated. "Now I know that's not the Potter house anymore. Alma Potter hated cats. Wouldn't even look at one if she could help it, much less set foot in the same house." She began to chuckle. "Next time those Thayer boys try teasing you, ask if they've ever heard of a witch afraid of cats."

Pam snapped the coin purse shut with her tooth safely inside and happily fitted the ring over her thumb, not a care in the world remaining.

But Pam had not seen that queer reflection in the window last night, nor how the window had gone instantly dark when Toby hissed at it—that same window that had fogged over this morning so not a shadow of a cat could be seen through it. Old magic and spells?

Kirsty's imagination was working overtime, she knew, but she was glad to leave Mrs. Vohl behind. Glad that this third side of the block was an uphill pull that called for concentration. Glad even to have a problem to wrestle with that was as down-to-earth ordinary as going back to school.

5

DEAR GRANDMA,

I can't believe it's been only fifteen days since I left Florida. It seems like I've been here a hundred years.

It was great to talk to you Sunday night, but I guess you could tell I couldn't say anything private. The phone here is in the hall, and anybody can listen. Pam stood right by me, listening, half the time and nobody made her stop. Nobody makes her do anything.

Kirsty scowled down at the tip of her pen before moving it on across the paper in front of her.

Today I finished my second week at Viktor Tweeten Middle School. How do you like that name? There are no steps or stairs in the building, which is the one good thing. The kids all act like a wheelchair is catching. Nobody talks to me but teachers.

Tomorrow is Saturday. I wish I could sleep in. I'm really tired. But Rita wants to take me shopping, so I suppose we will go shopping. I do need some winter clothes. I can't seem to get warm enough here even in bed with an extra blanket. Last night I dreamed a giant sponge was soaking up all the heat out of my body like I was a puddle it was mopping up.

That was only one of many nightmares that had invaded her sleep these past nights. Twice she had awakened in the dark, positive that someone was standing in her closet doorway whispering to her, wanting to be invited closer.

"Have you ever heard?" the whisper breathed in a coaxing singsong as if to entice a little kid in nursery school. "Have you ever heard . . . 'Tis a marvel of great renown!"

She kept on hearing it in her head even after she gathered the courage to snap on the bedside light and prove to herself that no one was there.

It was a struggle this very moment not to let her eyes slide toward the flowered curtains across the closet opening. She knew the curtains would be hanging perfectly straight anytime she looked at them directly, but she could not shake a crawly feeling that if she were quick enough with a sidelong glance, things might be otherwise.

She frowned down at the letter. Maybe she wouldn't be so bothered if there were someone she could talk to. Writing wasn't the same. Scrawled out on paper, the sponge dream sounded more like a goofy cartoon than a nightmare that had left her shuddering under the covers for nearly half an hour before she woke up.

But who was there to talk to who would listen? Certainly her breath was wasted when she had tried to persuade her father to let her have time—a week or two more, at least—to get used to the idea before she started school. "It's just not practical with Rita and me both gone all day," he had ended the discussion. "Besides, I should think you'd be as anxious as anybody to get back to normal as soon as can be." As if parading herself in a wheelchair in front of strangers in a strange school were "getting back to normal."

Kirsty tugged at the turtleneck of her sweater, pulling it up to her chin, although she doubted it would make her much warmer that way. The cold she felt seemed to come most from inside her, around the region of her heart.

Taking up the pen, she added, "I keep the picture of Mama and Gail and Daddy and me on the stand by my bed. It helps to look at it every day."

Knuckles banged a tattoo on the wall outside her room.

Pam's frowsy red thatch poked in past the edge of the door. "Hi."

Kirsty bent over her letter. "I'm busy."

"I'm looking for my tooth purse."

"Well, I don't have it," Kirsty said. One thing she did not need was a gaudy coin purse with someone's moldy old tooth inside.

The Tooth Fairy had duly left a dollar under Pam's pillow—apparently the going rate for teeth regardless of size—but had neglected to collect the tooth and its container. Pam had divided her time since then between mislaying the purse or, on finding it, taking the tooth out for inspection—most often it seemed and most revolting, at meal times.

"It could be under the dresser," Pam suggested, easing into the room.

"How could it be?" Kirsty asked. "How would it get there?" She pushed away from the desk as a half-formed suspicion blossomed into conviction. "You've been messing around in here by yourself, haven't you? That's how come I keep finding my tree candle pushed off-center."

"I don't push it anywhere," Pam said indignantly. "I always put it back right where it was."

Kirsty aimed a finger at her. "I told you never to touch it. And never is what I meant. *Never.*"

"I wouldn't hurt it. I only like to smell it." Pam's face was growing pink.

"Don't smell it. Don't touch it. Don't look at it."

"Okay, okay," Pam said, backing up. "I'm going to get one of my own just like it, anyway. Tomorrow, when we go shopping."

Kirsty snorted. "You can't. There isn't any other one just like it."

"Well, we're going to look and see." Pam's unimpressive chin lifted. "I've got my dollar, and Daddy's going to take me to a store that's all candles. All kinds."

Kirsty's eyes lost the power to blink. Her father wouldn't do such a thing. He knew how much that tree candle meant to her. He must. It was the one particular thing she had to remember Gail by. Her father wouldn't cheapen it by hunting up another just like it to hand over to Pam for a toy.

"Pam?" Rita called from the living room. "Here's your tooth purse. It was in Daddy's chair."

"Right." Pam was out the door at a run.

Kirsty did blink then, several times, her eyes returning to her letter. Slowly, deliberately, she drew rather than wrote in the space that remained:

LOVE,
KIRSTY

But the broad curves and swooping angles were not so large they could block out the image in her mind of her father watching TV last night, Pam wedged beside him in his chair as though she belonged there.

Quickly she folded the sheet of paper into thirds. Too quickly, for the edges were crooked, and she had to refold to bring them into line. She would have to ask her father for an envelope and stamp. And maybe ask him about his shopping plans for tomorrow as well.

She turned herself in the direction Pam had taken. If Rita was in the living room, chances were that was the place to find him, too.

No one was there, however, except Rita, jotting something on a notepad.

"Where's Daddy?" Kirsty asked, stopping in the archway.

"They went to round up his measuring tape and the calculator." Rita added a scribble to the pad. "Your father doesn't trust my brand of math."

"They," naturally, meant Pam was tagging along with him as usual.

"Is there something I can help you with?" Rita asked.

"No, that's okay. I'll wait for my dad." Kirsty started to move back. She wasn't comfortable when it was just her and Rita alone together. Perhaps that was Rita's feeling, too, for she merely nodded and turned away.

Kirsty paused, astonished to see her step up on a kitchen chair pulled close to the windows. "What are you doing?"

"Measuring for drapes. The trouble is, whoever built this place must have done it by-guess-and-by-gosh. No two of these windows measures exactly the same."

"Drapes? You mean like to pull across so you can't see out?" The idea sent a shock wave clear down to Kirsty's toes.

"They'll make the room a lot cozier at night, don't you think?" Rita was laying a yardstick over the space between the first two windows. "Warmer, too. I love this wavy old glass, but it's not the greatest for keeping in the heat."

But nighttime was when Kirsty wanted especially to see every inch of that wavy old glass. She couldn't count how often she glanced up to check on that farther window each evening. If that strange reflection had appeared in it once—twice, actually—might it not happen again? Some night when the lighting was precisely right, or her angle of vision, or even the sheen of snow falling outside?

"You can't cover them over with drapes. Drapes would be horrible."

"On tall windows like these? They need something to dress them up. They're so bare." Rita shifted her footing on the chair to look the row of windows up and down. "A deep, rich color in a fairly heavy, rich fabric? Don't you think that would add a touch of elegance?"

"No way!" Kirsty was startled by her own vehemence. She hadn't known until now how much she had been hoping for that shadowy door to reappear and give her a chance to see better what lay beyond it. But imagine explaining that to anyone.

Reckessly, she added, "Daddy hates drapes. He hates windows he can't see out of."

That wasn't a total invention. He had said something very like that once when she was nine and he made her remove the dozen transparent decals she had pasted on the dining-room window for their rainbow effect when the sun shone through.

"Hates drapes?" Rita repeated. "Gene? He hasn't said anything about it."

The answer was on Kirsty's tongue like words dictated from somewhere else. "You're newlyweds. He wouldn't want to hurt your feelings."

"Are you sure?" Puckers of doubt were gathering around Rita's eyes. Could it be that Rita was not so self-confident as she tried to appear?

"Charge!" Pam yelled, bursting into the room brandishing a length of metal tape measure like a wobbly sword.

Gene Hamilton came behind her. "Kirsty, you're here. Good." He handed her a pocket calculater. "You can help out with the math."

"Oh, look," Pam squealed.

Toby was in midair, leaping in pursuit of the tape. Laughing, Pam flicked it away from him. He did a graceful somersault, and was airborne again as soon as his feet touched the floor.

"Mommy, look. Daddy, did you see?" Pam let the tape retract into its case by fits and starts, reeling the cat toward her like a hooked fish.

"Kirsty, isn't he funny?"

He was, but Kirsty's grin was twisted by a jab of familiar pain between her eyes. Without planning to, she said shortly. " 'Tis a marvel of great reknown."

55

Pam giggled. "It's what?"

"It's part of a poem or something. 'Have you ever heard . . .'" Kirsty faltered, feeling foolish. "Never mind. I forget the rest." She had no idea what had compelled her to speak the senseless dream phrase. Nor, for that matter, why she should assume it was poetry.

" 'Have you ever heard of the Sugarplum Tree?' " Rita quoted. " ''Tis a marvel of great renown!' " She stepped down off the chair. "It's a poem by Eugene Field, I think. We have it in a book upstairs."

"I know that poem," Pam said. "I don't like it. You have to make a dog bark at the cat so it gets scared and runs around in the tree to shake the sugarplums down." She curled an arm about Toby, who was now on the couch, the better to keep an eye on the case into which he had seen the tape disappear. "I think it's a mean poem."

"It's a strange message for a children's poem when you put it that way," Rita agreed, laughing. "Stir up enough mayhem and you'll get sugarplums."

Nevertheless, it was a poem, a real poem that Kirsty might have heard anywhere and forgotten until it came floating to the surface in a dream. It wasn't just a fragment of a nightmare that wouldn't quit.

All at once it seemed easy to tell about her crazy dream. Maybe if the four of them laughed at it together, she wouldn't ever dream it again.

A second stab of pain derailed the impulse a moment, and the chance went by. Her father was holding his hand out for the measuring tape. "My turn now. Let's get this drapery business squared away."

"I don't know." Rita gave him a questioning glance. "Kirsty and I were talking. Maybe drapes aren't the best way to go."

"What's wrong with drapes?" he asked before Kirsty could think of a way to stall him. "I thought you wanted to get in on that sale of drapery goods tomorrow."

"I love drapes," Pam volunteered. "The kind that when you pull the rope they swoosh shut, and when you pull it again they swoosh open." She had to provide a dramatic demonstration, of course, jumping around and waving both arms. "Is that the kind we're going to get?"

Kirsty scowled at her. "Grow up. If you want to swoosh things, go play with the shower curtain."

"Kirsty," her father said warningly.

She fixed her eyes on him, willing him to be on her side for a change. "Drapes are ugly. We never had our windows covered at home. Mom never put up drapes."

"This is home, Kirsty," he said, spacing the words carefully. "Rita's and mine and Pam's and yours. The decorating in this house is Rita's department."

"But that's the thing." Rita laid a hand on his arm. "It's *our* house—our home, all four of us—so we ought to take everybody's likes and dislikes into consideration. There are other window ideas in that decorating book I had. The trouble is, I took the book with me this morning and left it at work."

57

"We could go get it," Pam said eagerly. "It's not that far. Let's."

"No," Kirsty's father cut in sharply. "No unnecessary driving on snowy streets after dark."

He was thinking of the accident, Kirsty knew. It was after dark on a snowy street that her mother and Gail had been taken from him—and he had been left with only Kirsty, the difficult one. Did that account for the trace of anger in his voice?

"We can stop by tomorrow and pick it up while we're out," he told Pam more gently.

"Sure. Okay." Her briefly clouded face cleared. "We can take Kirsty in and show her the whirlpool and exercise stuff?"

All at once everyone was looking at Kirsty as if they were about to close in.

"No. No way. I'm not going in. I'll sit in the car." She pushed herself backward with all her might.

"Watch out for Toby," Pam shrieked. "Stop!"

Kirsty saw him, too. Still alert to the case containing the metal tape, he lay in ambush under the end table. His tail was stretched out straight behind him and directly in the path of Kirsty's wheel.

She pulled with both hands to brake. Instead, the wheels, usually so sluggish on the thick living-room carpet, spun through her fingers as if she had given them an extra thrust.

Toby screeched. He plunged, screeched and plunged

again to escape the weight that rolled onto his tail and halted.

Pam hurled herself at Kirsty. "Get off him! Get off. Move!"

Kirsty was trying, but her palms were suddenly sweaty. They slid on the wheels without gripping.

Her father reached her in two strides and lifted her and the chair up together.

Toby sprang free, paused in the archway to deliver a furious hiss, and fled up the stairs.

"You did that on purpose. I saw you," Pam accused through welling tears. "You're mean. You're a mean, mean person."

"I'm not. I didn't," Kirsty began, but Pam was racing up the stairs, crying, "Toby? Toby?"

"I'll help her find him," Rita said. "I doubt he's seriously hurt, the carpet's so thick, but—" For once her lips were thin and unsmiling.

Kirsty turned to her father, fighting tears of her own. "I didn't do it on purpose. I couldn't stop in time."

"I would hope so. You know how much Pam loves that cat." His mouth had hardened, too.

"Don't you believe me?" One thing he must know was that she had never lied to him.

He shook his head slowly. "I don't know what to believe, except that you haven't been working very hard to make life here agreeable for anyone, including yourself."

Something too tight inside Kirsty snapped. "Why can't

you ever be on my side? You always think she's okay and I'm not. Why don't you just call her Gail and be done with it?"

She hadn't known she was shouting until she stopped and the silence pressed in on her eardrums as if she were under water.

"I didn't know you felt that way about Gail," her father said finally. He turned and walked away.

Kirsty gazed after him in shock. She wasn't talking about Gail. She was talking about *him*. She was saying Pam was not her sister. Pam was not his child. She was. She should be the one who mattered to him most.

"I'm not a mean person," she whispered to herself. "I'm not mean. I'm not."

Tears were sliding down her face now, faster than she could wink them off, but she couldn't take refuge in her room. She didn't want to risk meeting anyone in the hall.

She moved forward across the room to the deeper shadows at the fireplace end. There the farther window reflected the lamplight as a mellow glow, almost like firelight.

It *was* firelight.

And there it was, the room mirrored as she had seen it that other time, the door that didn't exist in the real room standing ajar. No, it was more than ajar. This time the corner of the flowered sofa was distinctly visible, and hardly less distinct were the legs of someone sitting on it, waiting.

Strangely, Kirsty was not surprised. Yet she could feel

her heart thudding as though it would shake her to pieces. Its cadence shaped itself into words: Sugarplum. Sugarplum. Sugarplum . . .

Stir up enough mayhem and you'll get sugarplums?

A fire was burning in the reflected fireplace. The flames leaped up for an instant in a broad, beckoning grin. Then the images blurred, shifted, vanished. The reflection in the glass became only mellow lamplight—and the dark rounds of her own eyes grown huge.

6

PAM SLANTED a sullen glance at the new down-filled vest Kirsty wore to breakfast Sunday morning. "That's not for in the house. That's to wear outdoors."

Kirsty's shrug was no friendlier. "Show me the tag that says so."

She lifted her mug of hot cocoa in both hands so the rising steam could warm the tip of her nose. What good would this vest do outdoors when she was shivering inside it in the house? Its vivid cherry color was its warmest quality.

"You look dumb," Pam said, flatly.

Pam, Kirsty was learning, was not a forgiving soul once her anger was aroused. What would she be like if Toby had been really hurt?

Kirsty made a face at her. "I don't look as dumb as

you. At least I'm dressed. My grandma says it's trashy to run around in your night clothes after you get up."

Pam was in bunny slippers and a fuzzy, too-small robe which, at that, was a step up from her usual breakfast attire—bare feet and pajamas.

Kirsty's father cleared his throat. "Kirsty—"

Rita, making French toast at the stove, was in robe and slippers, too. One more demerit for Kirsty.

She took a careful sip of her cocoa. What did it matter beside the score he already had chalked up against her?

"Anyone for more toast?" Rita asked cheerily as if she hadn't heard a thing. "Pam, you're not eating."

Pam stirred her fork in the soggy mess of syrup and toast on her plate. "I'm not real hungry. I ate some."

"Plus how many candy bars while we were shopping yesterday?" Rita asked. "And potato chips and corn curls? I warned you."

It was Kirsty's guess that Pam was suffering from a case of the sulks as well. She hadn't missed a store on the mall yesterday in her quest for a candle like Kirsty's, but in the end she had come away empty-handed. She and Kirsty's father had also checked out the gift shop of the nursing home while Rita collected the decorating book from her office, and while Kirsty sat stubbornly outside in the car, slowly freezing. There were no more tree-shaped candles to be had.

"Maybe a run out to the curb to pick up the newspaper would perk up your appetite," Kirsty's father suggested.

"I saw the boy go by a while ago, so it must be here."

Pam pulled her robe tighter. "It's cold out there."

"Not so cold," Rita said. "Run fast and you won't even feel it. That woolly robe should keep you plenty warm."

Kirsty watched Pam slide reluctantly off her chair and shuffle from the kitchen. She didn't even let the front door bang as she went out. Ordinarily she would be knocking the house down in her eagerness to do Kirsty's father a favor. Something wasn't right with her today, that was certain.

Kirsty's father added syrup to another piece of toast. "I wonder if that boy would deliver to the door if I offered him something extra to make it worth his while."

He was not asking Kirsty's opinion, and she did not volunteer it. Since Friday night they had been at pains to say as little as necessary to one another.

Her opinion would not please him in any case. "That boy" was Alf Thayer, and she doubted her father could afford the amount that would make it worth Alf's while to deliver to the door of this house. Alf's method was to swerve his bike in fast from across the road, thrust the paper into its tube beside the mailbox, and swerve away again as if a skinny arm might rise out of nowhere to grab him if he got too close. He wasn't about to stumble into any old magic or leftover spells if he could help it.

What would really finish her with her father was that she wasn't so sure anymore that Alf was all that far off-base. There was something strange about this house.

She could tell herself the images in the window had a

64

logical explanation. She could tell herself it was coincidence that on both evenings when she saw those images she had been the cause of sudden discord in the midst of everyone's sweet harmony. She could call herself crazy for even wondering if the images were her "sugarplums" for "stirring up mayhem."

But she could not tell herself she had purposely run over Toby. She had not. Her chair had. Something had wrenched the chair out of her control and sent her wheeling viciously backward. Something for which she had no explanation. Just remembering the sensation made her mouth dry.

She looked over the rim of her mug at her father. Once upon a time she could have told him anything, and he would have listened seriously and given her a serious answer. If now he would only give her a smile . . .

"Kirsty," he said, not smiling, "Rita asked you a question."

Rita nodded. "I asked if the paperboy doesn't ride the school bus with you."

"Yes," Kirsty said. "But he never talks to me." From her observation, Alf was not big on talking to any girl if someone else was around, but she couldn't keep an accusing note from her voice. "Nobody talks to me."

"Have you tried talking to them?" her father asked. "You can't always leave it to the other guy to move first."

So once more the fault was hers for not trying harder.

She retreated to the bathroom after breakfast. As she maneuvered her chair into the cramped space between the door and the sink, Toby jumped onto the counter. He settled himself expectantly to enjoy the spectacle of water trickling from a faucet and vanishing down a drain.

Kirsty reached out to pet him before adjusting the flow to suit them both and squeezing the toothpaste onto her brush. Her chair had done no real damage to his tail, and he was the one creature in the house apparently willing to forget the whole incident.

"Hey, I want to get in there," Pam yelled at the door. She banged it against the back of the chair.

"Can't," Kirsty said through a mouthful of foam. "No room." That was surely self-evident. "Go upstairs."

"I can't. Daddy's up there." Pam tried to squeeze by the wheelchair and failed. "Get out of the way. I want to get in."

"Wait your turn," Kirsty said. She saw no reason to hurry.

Pam's small face contorted. "This isn't your private bathroom. Just because Daddy put up bars and stuff for you to hang onto doesn't mean it's only for you. You better move so I can get in."

"Or else what? You'll send the big, bad witch to get me?" Kirsty wished the words unsaid before they were out. Why did witches keep popping into her mind?

"Maybe I'll turn into a witch myself and get you." Pam uttered a witchy cackle so full of malice that Kirsty turned her head to be sure the sound actually came from her.

Toby crooked a paw at the column of water from the

faucet and tried with a quick move to pull it toward him. Drops spattered in every direction.

Pam screeched as if she were burned. "Stop it. Stop it! You get out of here!" She snatched a towel from the rack and whipped him to the floor with it.

"Pam!" Rita was in the hallway, gazing at them in shock.

Pam lowered her arm, the fury dying from her face, leaving it a yellowish tinge that gave her freckles the look of a dusting of red pepper. "I don't care. He scared me. He doesn't belong there."

Rita shook her head, frowning. "You're not making sense. What are you talking about?"

Pam wilted into tears. "I don't know. I don't feel good. I'm so cold."

Rita drew her into the hall and pressed a hand against Pam's forehead. "You feel hot to me. Let's go get the thermometer."

They went up the stairs, Pam whimpering, Rita murmuring reassurances.

Kirsty screwed the cap on the toothpaste with fingers a bit shaky. Whether or not Toby had scared Pam, Pam had scared her. Those pale green eyes had been as glassy and unfocused as marbles when they glared at her and the cat. Like a zombie's. Hate.

Toby was nowhere to be seen, and who could blame him? He must think Kirsty and Pam both had joined the ranks of Alma Potter, the cat-hating old woman. Trust

Pam, though, to end up the center of sympathy after willfully hitting him, while Kirsty, who had had no desire to hurt him, remained unexcused and unforgiven.

Proof of that, if she needed it, was hers a little later as she sat alone in the living room, idly shifting channels with the TV remote control. During a station-break lull in the program chatter, Rita's voice came to her from the kitchen:

"I can't imagine what possessed her. That's not like Pam to be rough with any animal. And now she's sound asleep. She does have a slight temp, but nothing I'd ordinarily think was alarming—"

"Probably she's just worn out," Kirsty's father said. "All that running around yesterday wore me out, and she's been operating at full throttle for over a week. Kids' nerves can frazzle, too, you know." He exhaled a highly audible sigh. "Let's face it: life hasn't been exactly stress-free around here lately."

Poor innocent little Pam. Poor everyone except Kirsty. She didn't stay to hear more.

In her room, she snapped a cassette into her tape player on the desk and crammed the earphones over her ears.

The desk drawer, standing partly open, dug a corner into her knee. She gave the drawer an angry shove, but it was jamming somehow. A jerk, another shove and a jerk, and it came loose to display a jumble of pencils and crayons spilled from their boxes, a bent folder, wrinkled notebook pages.

A sheet of stiff paper, drawing paper, shot off the top into her lap. It was the witch sketch she had made the day after her arrival, then buried facedown under a drawing pad and forgotten.

Who had been rummaging in this drawer? As if she had to ask. Poor, innocent Pam, indeed.

The witch face leered up at her, a crude line drawing every bit as baleful and ugly as she remembered it.

Yet, not exactly as she remembered. She would have said she had sketched it in profile, but here it was, its knowing smirk presented full-front. More remarkable, those hasty strokes of her crayon had somehow achieved a three-dimensional effect—as if the face were a thing separate from the paper on which it rested.

Kirsty felt her scalp tightening. She knew that face. She had actually seen it somewhere, not long ago.

This morning—

In the bathroom—

Pam's face.

No matter that the hollows and ridges of the witch face were hardly a mirror image of Pam's button features. This morning Pam's face had been twisted in that same venomous mask.

Rita was puzzled by what could have possessed her. What if the answer were in the question? Possessed.

No way. Forget that kind of thinking.

Kirsty began to wiggle the drawer back into its slot. Pam was the sort of kid who turned monster when she got sick. Simple as that.

Furthermore, she was lucky to be sick, for she was going to want all the sympathy she could recruit when Kirsty confronted her with this trashed drawer.

She was about to return the witch drawing to its place on top when it occurred to her that her cause would not be helped any if her father saw this sketch. Best rid herself of it while she could.

Again, as before, the paper resisted her attempt to rip it. It was not proof against crushing, though. She crumpled it into as small and tight a ball as she could make it and pitched it into the wicker wastebasket.

It came over her that she did not feel too well, either. She bent her head on her crossed arms while a rush of dizziness eddied around her.

"Okla-homa, Okla-homa," a chorus of mixed voices sang through her earphones . . . Or was it just one voice she was hearing, whispery and old, crooning words of its own to her in the cadence of the music? "Coming—for you. Coming—for you—" The voice of her nightmares.

She struggled to push off the earphones, to raise her head, but it was as if her bones had turned to sand.

She knew she must be dozing, dreaming. Knew that all she had to do was wake up. If she could.

"Coming—for you—"

The tape played to its end, and with a snap, the machine switched itself off. At once the fog in her brain thinned and fled.

The earphones were lying on the desk, silent. No surging music. No rasping whisper. She was awake.

She straightened up to discover Toby crouched in front of her beside the tape player. Where had he come from?

She flexed her fingers, wondering at how stiff they felt and cold. As if she had been outdoors for a long time without mittens.

A fine line of blood was welling across the ball of the middle finger. Had the cat scratched her?

But, no, he wasn't even looking at her. He was peering down over the edge of the desk.

Kirsty followed his stare.

The wastebasket lay on its side, and the wadded-up witch sketch had rolled onto the floor. Only it wasn't wadded up anymore. The creases had unfolded and relaxed until the sly gray face was grinning up at her once more.

It was the sketch that had slashed her finger. She remembered now. A razor edge of that paper when she had crushed it.

She was seized by an urge to lean over and smear her bleeding finger across that bloodless grin. Fresh blood. Wouldn't that give it something to grin about?

Before she could act, Toby hurled himself down on the sketch, pouncing as if he suspected a mouse to be lurking underneath.

Startled, Kirsty detoured the injured finger to her own mouth, and the impulse to share her blood left her.

She thought she heard a noise near her feet, like a faint cry or a squeak. It had to be the sound of cat claws puncturing crisp paper, yet—

Kirsty shuddered, feeling like a person who had narrowly missed blundering onto a snake coiled to strike.

7

SPATTERS OF RAIN were changing to pellets of sleet when the school bus drew up in front of Viktor Tweeten Middle School on Monday morning.

Kirsty, in her seat by the door, watched the stream of kids pouring past her and out. Some threw her sidelong glances as they left. A few openly stared. Most kept their eyes straight ahead, never once letting them stray her way. How did her father think she could just strike up a conversation with any of them whenever she chose?

"Okay," Mr. Gabel, the driver, boomed above her after the last kid hit the pavement. "How's about a great big hug now? Nice and tight."

She cringed at the grandstand performance he always made of lifting her on or off the bus. He would not even try to carry her unless she were practically strangling him. At that, he did such a clumsy, staggering job of it that she was never certain whether he was clowning or on the verge of actually letting her fall.

At least there was less of an audience standing around this morning to gawk. The raw wind and spitting sleet were sending most people scurrying into the building. Hardly anyone was left but Alf Thayer, who pushed her chair into place under her as Mr. Gabel swooped her down with a resounding "Alley-oop!"

Three different times last week Mr. Gabel had asked for help from the boys in figuring out how to fold or unfold her chair, and each time Alf was among the volunteers. Somehow, in the process, Alf had become unofficial Keeper of the Chair. The mechanics of it were what interested him, however, and not any inclination to socialize. He was generally off to join his pals at the front door before she got her backpack squared on her shoulders.

It was a surprise to find him scuffing alongside her today up the broad walk to the school.

"Guess who I seen yesterday scooting around with a walker," he said, not looking at her. "Old Lady Potter. She's up and out of bed."

Sleet stung Kirsty's face like a slap. "Where were you, to see her?"

"At the home—Custer Manor. I deliver papers there. She wasn't even in a chair like yours. She's getting places with a walker."

Kirsty tried to convey scorn with her chin dug into

her collar and ice-melt sliding down her cheeks. "Is that supposed to scare me?"

Alf raised a tattered notebook between himself and the peppering wind. "It would scare me if I was living in her house. All of a sudden she's getting her batteries charged up from somewhere. Somehow."

"We don't live in *her* house. We live in *our* house." Kirsty hunched forward to pick up speed. This was one conversation she did not need.

"Sure," Alf said, keeping pace. "How is everything at *your* house? Nobody acting sick or under the weather or like that?"

"Everybody is fine," Kirsty said decidedly.

Maybe "fine" was not an exact description of Pam's puffy lids and pasty complexion this morning, but Rita had judged her well enough to go to school. "Everybody is fine, and Halloween is over."

"Right. So she don't have much time before Christmas if she's going to make her move." He loped a step ahead of her to pull open the heavy front door. "Spells and stuff don't work at Christmas season, you know," he added as he took off down the hall.

She did not know. Neither did she much care. Christmas was what stuck in her mind as she headed for her locker. Not much time before Christmas . . .

Up to now she had been doing pretty well at blocking out the fact that another Christmas was closing in on her. Last year she had been at Grandma Pollard's where the

Florida setting was so unreal—colored lights twinkling among the fronds of palm trees and people in sandals and shorts strolling underneath—that the carols and decorations were more like the props of an elaborate theme party she was not obliged to attend.

It would not be that painless this year. Rita would be pretending they were one cozy, happy family, and Pam would demand all the trimmings from reindeer-shaped cookies to a star at the top of a real Christmas tree—just as Gail and Kirsty always used to do. And Kirsty would be expected to behave as if she never noticed they were all the wrong people in the wrong place. She wished she could crawl inside her locker and hibernate until after New Year's.

She was in third-hour study hall, doodling palm leaves across the top of her folder, before she thought about what else Alf had said. Did he seriously suppose she would believe that some creepy old woman in a nursing home was mysteriously gaining strength by draining energy from her and Pam? Probably that would be his explanation of why Kirsty was never warm anymore. She could imagine him saying, too, that maybe she had set the whole machinery in operation herself when she had wished so hard for a magical escape into the past her first evening in Alma Potter's magic-steeped house. For that matter, she could imagine him saying anything he thought might bother a person or spoil their sleep.

She cast a glance around the study hall, so reassuringly ordinary, full of ordinary kids doing ordinary things—

some reading, some writing, some looking bored, and one creating a ripple of giggles with a hefty sneeze. A Thanksgiving poster done in tones of bronze and gold was tacked to the bulletin board. Thanksgiving was only three days off.

Did witches, like department stores, count the day after Thanksgiving as the start of the Christmas season?

Sleet was still ticking against the windows. A pebbly, pale gray surface was building up on the outer sill, looking nasty and cold. She wished whoever was in charge of heat in this school would turn the temperature up a half-dozen notches. By lunchtime the grainy sleet layer had disappeared beneath a thickening cover of snow. Instead of stampeding for the cafeteria when the passing buzzer sounded at the end of English class, a handful of students collected at the windows.

"Oh, no," mourned a girl in a coral sweatshirt. "Look how it's piling up. And I have to walk home tonight."

"Yay, snow," cheered one of the boys. "We get a snow day tomorrow, I bet."

The term was new to Kirsty, waiting for the lunch-hour rush in the halls to thin. "Snow day?" she ventured. "What is that?"

She doubted anyone would answer.

The girl closest to her—a tall blonde called Amber—jumped as if a desk had spoken. She looked over her shoulder and as quickly looked away. Then she turned and, for perhaps the first time, looked at Kirsty straight on. "It's when they call off school because there's too much snow." Unexpectedly, she smiled. "I guess you're not from Wisconsin."

Kirsty shook her head. "Florida. And Ohio."

The coral sweatshirt girl turned, too. "Do you really live in the Potter house?"

Kirsty had no chance to reply. A voice from the doorway cut in. "Boys? Girls? What are you congregating here for? You belong in the lunchroom."

Mrs. Vohl, trim in a gray suit and lavender blouse, flapped her hands at them, shooing them like chickens. They shooed, laughing as they scattered, the way Alf and Dean had done the day of the snowball fight. Only Amber hesitated, as if she wanted to say something more.

Mrs. Vohl flapped her away. "Hurry up. Get going. We have things to do, if you don't."

She beamed at Kirsty across the emptied room when Amber was gone. "Ready to go? I think the worst of the mad dash is over."

Last week a teacher's aide had been assigned to help Kirsty fill her lunch tray and transport it safely to a table, but on the second day, Mrs. Vohl had taken over, explaining, "We're new neighbors. We need to get better acquainted." She was good at moving Kirsty briskly through the cafeteria line and never failed to find her an unpopulated spot where she could eat, no matter how crowded the tables were.

Come to think of it, Kirsty reflected as she glimpsed Amber and the coral sweatshirt turn a corner together at the far end of the corridor, Mrs. Vohl seemed to have a fondness for clearing other people out of the way.

Today everyone in the lunchroom appeared to be in a hurry to eat and get outside to check out the weather. Kirsty heard "snow day" on every side.

"There wasn't a word about snow in the forecast last night," Mrs. Vohl said, watching Kirsty sample what the school menu listed as "hamburger hot dish." "I should have suspected, though. Ever since I was a little girl, I've always had a different sort of headache when there's a freak storm brewing."

She pressed her fingertips to a spot above her eyes.

The gesture was so like Kirsty's own when that strange, probing pain attacked behind and between her eyes that she winced in sympathy.

Mrs. Vohl patted her on the shoulder. "Don't let it worry you, sweetie. It's mostly my imagination, according to the doctors, and it could be they're right. I know I'll forget it as soon as I find something else to think about."

She was oddly still for a while, staring into space as if listening for inspiration on some private receiver.

"Finished?" she asked when Kirsty drained the last swallow from her milk carton. "I think then I'll phone your people and let them know I can bring you home a little early if they like. No telling how late the school buses may be if this snow keeps on."

It did keep on, and an hour later Mr. Neale, the school

custodian, was lifting Kirsty into Mrs. Vohl's minivan. Snow lay an inch deep on every twig, branch, and wire, looking as delicate as foam, but the evergreens beside the front entrance were beginning to droop under the weight.

Beneath the snow the streets were icy, and Mrs. Vohl took a roundabout route that avoided going up the steep hill to the brick house. The minivan was turning the last corner when Kirsty realized, "I don't have a key."

"You won't need one. Your little sister is home already. The elementary children were dismissed at noon."

Did that mean that Pam, age nine, was trusted with a key while Kirsty, going on fourteen, was not? She scowled. "We aren't sisters."

"I know," said Mrs. Vohl, undisturbed. "But she's such a little sweetheart, isn't she? It was so cute Saturday when she walked in and saw we had a whole pile of those pumpkin-purse key rings on the counter in the gift shop. She just had to show me she had hers right with her and that, sure enough, her tooth was still inside."

"You work in a gift shop?" Kirsty asked, rather than comment on Pam's cuteness. "At the mall?"

"At Custer Manor. I volunteer two days a month there."

Custer Manor again. Kirsty wondered if she were the only person in town who had not been in that place this weekend—her father and Pam, Rita, Mrs. Vohl, Alf—and Alma Potter.

She clutched the armrest as the minivan came to a sliding stop in the driveway.

"I have to learn not to chatter so much when I'm on an errand," Mrs. Vohl said severely, yet in a queer little voice like a child repeating a reprimand.

She unloaded Kirsty's chair and helped her into it with none of Mr. Gabel's dramatics—more evidence of her nursing home experience, perhaps. Kirsty was glad of her help in wheeling up the ice-covered ramp to the kitchen door, which a sour-faced Pam took her own time in opening for them.

How long did this kid hang onto a grudge, Kirsty wondered.

"I was in the basement," Pam said before anyone could ask. "I didn't hear you."

Mrs. Vohl sank into a kitchen chair as soon as she was inside, the back of her gloved hand pressed to her eyes. "I wonder— Do you have any headache remedy in the house?"

"There's some stuff my mom always takes. It's in the bathroom cabinet down there." Pam pointed to the hall. She did not rush off to do the fetching herself in her usual fashion.

Mrs. Vohl found her own way, and emerged a few minutes later looking a touch less strained. "I can tell somebody cares a lot about you," she nodded at Kirsty. "It took a good deal of thought and hard work to fit up a bathroom so nicely for you. I can remember when that space was only a big storage closet under the stairs."

Pam was surprised out of her sulks. "When were you ever in our house?"

"Years ago, when I was about your age. I started out one summer to be Miss Potter's errand girl. I was so proud she wanted me. She had been my kindergarten teacher, you know. Besides, I was dying to get inside this old house and look around." Mrs. Vohl sighed regretfully. "Then my parents decided I needed a change of scene, and shipped me off to my grandparents in Kansas for the rest of the summer."

"How come?" Pam asked.

Mrs. Vohl was gazing around her, taking in everything—the length of the hall, the height of the ceiling, the living-room archway.

"It was a doctor's idea mainly. He insisted. I was having headaches he couldn't explain and too many nightmares to suit him." She moved on into the living room as she spoke. "Miss Potter took it all very personally, I remember."

Pam drifted alongside her. "You mean she was mad at you?"

Mrs. Vohl chuckled. "She was mad at Dr. Miller. He was pressuring the school board to force her to quit teaching. He said the records would prove she was considerably older than she claimed and years beyond retirement age."

"Did he get her fired?" Kirsty didn't much care, but she wanted to get off the topic of headaches. The power of suggestion was beginning to drive tiny darts of pain behind her own eyes.

"No, poor man, he was killed by lightning that summer. On the golf course. There were some terrible storms that year. Lightning struck the school administration building, too, and burned it to the ground, records and all."

"Lucky for Miss Potter," Kirsty said.

"Yes. Miss Potter went right on teaching for about another twenty years. So far as I know, nobody else ever tried to stop her."

Kirsty did a quick calculation in her head. If retirement age were sixty-five, and if Miss Potter had taught, say five years beyond it before the doctor's challenge, she would have been seventy at the time. Twenty years more would mean she was still teaching at the age of ninety. Some of Mrs. Vohl's stories, when examined, were as fantastic as Alf Thayer's.

"Well, my goodness. Look at this." Mrs. Vohl had spotted the book of children's verse Rita had brought downstairs yesterday and left on an end table. "Eugene Field. Talk about reviving old memories."

She was at the table, switching on the lamp as she picked up the book. The glow of light in the gloom filtering in from outside through falling snow drew Pam and Kirsty toward her like an invitation.

" 'Wynken, Blynken and Nod,' " she crooned, flipping the pages. " 'The Gingham Dog and the Calico Cat,' . . . Oh, and 'The Sugarplum Tree.' Miss Potter read her kindergartners all of these, but that was her favorite."

She tilted her head, eyes half closed: " 'Have you ever heard of the Sugarplum Tree?' "

Kirsty's heart stumbled on a beat, then raced to catch up with itself. That poem was probably a favorite of hundreds of people. There was nothing so weird about Alma Potter being one of them.

" 'You say but the word to that gingerbread dog,' " Mrs. Vohl half read, half recited, " 'And he barks with such terrible zest/That the chocolate cat is at once all agog'—"

Kirsty wanted to hear no more. "Siccing a dog on the cat," she interrupted. "Probably that was the part she liked best. You said she hated cats."

"Was afraid of them," Mrs. Vohl corrected. "Although I suppose it amounts to the same thing in the end—hating and being afraid."

"Would she hurt Toby if she caught him, do you think?" Pam asked. "Dean says witches like to turn cats into familiars. He said she might do that to Toby if she got him."

"Make Toby a familiar? You mean like a servant to do secret errands for her and ride along on her broomstick?" A silly picture rose in Kirsty's mind of Toby running an errand, trotting up the walk with a rolled newspaper as big as he was clamped in his jaws.

"Dean says familiars can be anything, like a dog or a crow or a person, even. But mostly witches choose cats."

Kirsty's mental picture became sillier—Mrs. Vohl on all fours, gripping the newspaper in her teeth.

Mrs. Vohl closed the book and put it down. "I promise you Alma Potter's one interest in your cat is to keep as much distance between him and herself as possible. He's such a nice kitty cat, too. He and I have been getting acquainted lately since he's discovered the catnip patch behind my garage."

Her gaze wandered over the room. It traced the row of windows, brushed across the fireplace, moved to the sofa and paused. It wasn't the sofa she was studying, Kirsty realized; it was the expanse of wall above it—that same expanse that drew Kirsty's eyes so often in search of what was not there.

"Is this room changed from how it used to be?" Kirsty hoped it sounded like a natural, ordinary question.

Mrs. Vohl started, like someone roused on the brink of dozing off. "There was a box of puppets on a shelf," she said oddly. "Storybook people the kindergartners liked."

Another pause while she studied the wall. "That was one of those nightmares I had so long ago. I was in this room, dancing. I didn't want to dance. I wanted to go home, and I was crying. But she kept making me jump higher and farther and faster and faster, and I couldn't stop because I was one of her puppets and she could make me do whatever she said."

"She? Miss Potter?" Kirsty asked.

A gust of wind rattled the windows, and Mrs. Vohl drew back a step. "Did I say 'she'? I don't know who it was. It was just a dream a long time ago."

She was massaging her forehead again. "I'm talking too much. Staying too long. I better be on my way."

She was on her way as she spoke, heading for the kitchen as if unseen hands were shoving her. She retrieved her handbag from the table, patted Kirsty's cheek, Pam's head, and wrestled the storm door open.

There she stopped. "This isn't right. I shouldn't be leaving you girls here alone like this. Promise me you won't—"

The wind tore the door from her hand and sent her skidding and sliding down Kirsty's ramp. Another gust slammed the door shut on whatever it was she would have had them promise.

8

KIRSTY WATCHED through the kitchen window until the white minivan pulled out of the driveway. It appeared to vanish into the swirling snow mist when it reached the street. The veil of snow thickened and drew in closer around the house like a curtain shutting it away from the rest of the world.

Pam watched, too, leaning her head against the pane. "She's a crazy lady," she said without particular emphasis when Mrs. Vohl was gone.

"Nice," Kirsty said, beginning to push away from the window. "She thinks you're a little sweetheart."

Pam turned her head to stick out her tongue. "She's a crazy lady," she repeated more firmly. "She even told Dean's daddy so one time when he gave her a ride home because her car broke down on the bridge. She told him she was trying to run away because she does stuff that makes her cry afterward but she can't ever remember what it was. Only that it's bad."

"Mrs. Vohl does bad stuff?" In Kirsty's opinion if Mrs. Vohl had a problem it was her determination to do *good* stuff, whether anybody wanted it done or not. Like always shooing off kids before they could get too close to Kirsty.

"Dean says she could be in somebody's power. Like she could be a familiar."

Kirsty laughed. "I'll tell you who the crazy person is: Dean. You, too, for listening to him when you know how dumb he is."

Dean's brother, Alf, could also qualify for that list she reflected as she wheeled out of the kitchen. Alf and his witch with a walker, marshalling her forces for the big move.

Ahead of Kirsty, the gleam of light from the living room blazed bright suddenly, flickered, and sank back to a soft gleam. Her first thought was of fire, flames leaping in the fireplace—a fire that had no reason to be there.

She rushed forward through the archway to find the room no different from how she had left it ten minutes ago, except that the gloom was perhaps a degree or two deeper. At the far end, the empty fireplace gaped cold and shadowy in the half-dark beyond the glow of the lamp Mrs. Vohl had switched on.

It must have been the lamp that blazed and flickered. The storm was playing tricks with the power.

Kirsty sat waiting for her heart to slow down. At the

same time she grew aware of how still the house had become, as if it were waiting for something, too. That was silly, she told herself impatiently. Rita should be home before long to take charge of things. She was always here by the time the school bus delivered Kirsty at quarter past three.

In the meantime there was no reason just to sit here, staring at space and feeling creepy.

Kirsty made herself move forward to the lamp beside her father's chair. What this place needed was more light.

When she added the lamps at either end of the sofa, the last of the shadows fled. As she drew back to approve the change, she was facing the wall that had appeared to catch Mrs. Vohl's special attention.

Kirsty narrowed her eyes, trying to picture the overall layout of the house. Where would a door in that wall lead? Into her bedroom. Into the back of her closet, to be more exact. So much for that theory. Who would want a door from the living room into a bedroom closet?

"What are you doing?" Pam asked, trailing in to flop herself across the arm of Gene Hamilton's chair.

"Nothing." Kirsty picked up the TV remote control and pressed ON. The set responded with a roar of sandpapery noise and a screen of churning particles.

"The cable's gone out," Pam said as if she were rather pleased to be the bearer of ill news. "It always goes when there's a storm."

Kirsty tried two more channels by way of judging for herself, and shut the set off. Shut off, shut in, muttered a still-edgy part of her mind as the screen went blank.

She looked away from the set and up, searching for a different thought. It occurred to her that she had no idea how the upstairs was laid out. "What room is up there?" she asked, pointing to the ceiling. "Right over us, I mean."

"I don't know. Daddy's and my mom's bedroom, I guess." Pam squinted at the ceiling. "Or maybe the dark closet."

"What's the dark closet?"

"It's a big, dark closet with no light inside and lots of shelves and drawers and stuff. I'm not supposed to go in it alone because the door sticks."

"And you never do what you're not supposed to, right?" Kirsty said, the mention of drawers bringing to mind her wrath of yesterday. "Like sneak into my room again and trash my desk drawer? I'm showing it to my dad tonight exactly the way you left it, so you better start thinking up a good way to explain it."

Pam sat blinking at her. "What drawer? I don't know about any drawer."

Her bewilderment was almost believable. But that would mean the mischief had been done by someone else. Or by some *thing* . . . Kirsty was not about to be tempted down that line of thought.

"Maybe you just don't remember, like Mrs. Vohl," she suggested, her anger building. "Maybe you trash other people's stuff and forget about it, the way you're always forgetting where you left that silly tooth purse."

"My tooth purse is right here." Pam dug into her sweater pocket and produced it with a flourish. "And here's my tooth."

Triumphant, she turned the purse over. She turned it a second time, turned it around. Her grin faded.

"Pinch your finger?" Kirsty asked, resolved not to back off from the unappetizing tooth when it was thrust at her.

"Where's the snap thing that shuts it?" Pam asked. "It's only got that sticking stuff. It never had that stuff before."

"What are you talking about?"

Pam put the purse into Kirsty's hand. "Look how it closes."

Kirsty saw what she meant. There was no trace of the metal clasp that had opened and closed the little purse. There was only a strip of Velcro.

"This isn't your tooth purse," she said after a moment's baffled staring. "It's even a different color. Yours is bright orange, and this one is practically yellow."

"It is too my tooth purse. I never even took it out of my pocket since we got home from shopping Saturday." Pam's voice jumped up an octave. "How could it get changed?"

"Stop. Take a deep breath and think," Kirsty said. It was the advice her father used to give her and Gail whenever a puzzle appeared to be beyond solution. She drew a deep breath herself, and like a waiting bubble, the logical explanation bobbed to the surface. "Listen. Mrs. Vohl showed you a whole bunch of these pumpkin purses in

91

the gift shop, right? And you were showing her your tooth. So you must have accidentally picked up the wrong purse when you left. Simple."

Pam glanced doubtfully from the purse to Kirsty's face to the purse again. "You mean my tooth purse is at the gift shop? What if someone buys it?" She clapped a hand to her mouth. "My tooth! What if the old witch that lives there finds it and makes a spell on me?"

The tooth lost on Saturday; Pam sick and vicious Sunday; anxious, edgy today— What if the purse swap were not pure accident? What if Mrs. Vohl really were a familiar, and through her the witch now possessed Pam's tooth and the power it gave her to work evil with it?

Kirsty tossed the purse into Pam's lap. "I'm sick of that witch stuff. It's a stupid game."

The lamplight dimmed around them. A brownish haze that was neither light nor darkness hung in the room for a second before the power returned in full.

Pam gave Kirsty a wise smile. "She heard you, and she didn't like it."

Kirsty drew another deep breath. "Why don't you go outside and play in the snow? Go build a snowman—a nice cat snowman to scare the wicked witch away."

A new thought struck her. "Where's Toby?" Ordinarily the cat was on hand to observe the arrival of each of them when they came home, but she could not recall seeing him anywhere this afternoon.

"I don't know. Upstairs asleep probably." Pam yawned.

"He's mad at me because I put him outdoors this morning."

"You put him out in all that nasty weather?" Kirsty was no expert on the care and nurture of cats, but that seemed an unlikely thing to do to a cherished pet, especially in a house she knew was equipped with a perfectly good litter box in the basement. "You let him in again, didn't you?"

Pam had wriggled herself down in the corner of the big chair to where her head rested on the chair arm. "I guess. I don't remember."

Her air of utter indifference sounded an alarm for Kirsty. "Are you getting sick again or something?"

Pam definitely did not look right, now that Kirsty really considered her. She looked cold, for one thing, huddled together in the chair. She looked smaller, too, as though she had shrunk a size or two overnight. But a person couldn't grow visibly thinner in the few hours between Sunday morning and Monday afternoon, could she?

Pam rolled her head slowly from side to side on the chair arm. "Why should I be sick?"

"Because the first thing you always do when you come home is go check out Toby."

"My mom turned down the heat when we left," Pam said dreamily to the ceiling. "First I had to go make it warmer."

As if pushing the thermostat up a couple of notches called for a major effort of mind and muscle. Whatever the effort, the house was not warm. Kirsty was regretting having left her outdoor jacket in the kitchen. The thermostat was just outside the living room. If she could stretch tall enough to reach it from her chair, why not set it up to where the furnace would deliver some real heat for a change?

That was how she happened to be in the hall and close enough to the phone to pick it up when it rang. "I've got it," she called out before Pam could launch her customary sprint to be the first to answer.

"Kirsty? You're home then. Good," came her father's voice over the wire. "The radio said the schools had been dismissed early, but I wanted to be sure. Is Pam home, too?"

"Yes," Kirsty said. Silly of her to think even for a moment that his main concern was only for her.

"Rita isn't there, is she?"

"No, not yet." Kirsty hunted for more to say that would keep him talking to her. At least he was speaking to her again. "Are you coming home soon?" She remembered he had mentioned at breakfast that he was scheduled to spend the day in a neighboring town.

"It doesn't look like it. There're a dozen stalled cars on the road up ahead, and right now nothing's moving in either direction. I'm about ten miles west of Frederiksen at the Red Pine Lodge. Can you remember that name?"

"Red Pine Lodge," she repeated. There was a hum on

94

this line like the rush of a distant waterfall that made it hard to hear exactly.

"Right. I tried to reach Rita, but their phone lines at Custer Manor are all tied up. Tell her not to fix supper for me. There's no knowing how late I may be. Is everything—"

The hum surged over his voice, drowning it out.

"Daddy?" she called into the receiver. "Daddy?"

"I'm here," he said as the hum subsided. "We better sign off, though, while the signal holds. Tell Pam there's a cat here marked just like Toby except it's gray."

A message for Pam, a message for Rita, but no special word for Kirsty. The hum was rising again as she said good-bye, and she hung up quickly.

"Is that Daddy?" Pam demanded, appearing beside her, hand out for the phone. "Let me talk."

"It was *my* daddy, and I talked," Kirsty said, pushing away from the wall niche that held the phone. "When it's your daddy, you can talk all you like."

"My real daddy? He won't ever call."

"Okay then, your mom," Kirsty snapped. "You've got a choice. Nobody in your family's dead."

It was the first she had used that word since the accident. Unaccountably, she felt she was going to cry.

Pam trudged slowly after her into the living room. "Did your mom want to die?"

"What kind of stupid question is that?" Kirsty asked, keeping her back turned.

"Was she glad to go away and leave you?" Pam persisted, her voice shrilling. "Because my daddy was. He went away on purpose because he didn't want us anymore."

Kirsty had no answer for that. Neither did she care to think about it, although she had a suspicion that it would wait for her somewhere until she did.

She paused to gaze through the nearest window at the dark smudges that were evergreens blurred by falling snow. The twinges of headache she had felt earlier were beginning to throb like a pulse beat.

Pam picked up yesterday's newspaper from a footstool, and returned to her nook in the armchair with it. "I wish my mom would get home. I don't like it here without her."

Kirsty switched on the stereo. This house was too quiet.

The voice of the local FM announcer came on, reeling off highways and roads that were "snow-covered and slippery," "in poor winter driving condition," or simply "hazardous." He followed that with a list of cancelled activities—Boy Scout meetings, the Civic Band rehearsal, the Friends of the Library dinner, tryouts for the community theater . . .

She was about to spin the dial to something more lively when the announcer interrupted himself. "Hold on, folks. I've just been handed a note. An elderly patient has apparently wandered away from Custer Memorial Manor. She is wearing a dark coat and walking with two canes.

Police and staff members are searching the area. If you see this person, please get her in out of the storm and call Custer Memorial Manor or the Frederiksen police. The name is Alma Potter, but she may be too confused to respond to it. Let me repeat—"

Kirsty heard the bulletin through a second time without moving a muscle even to breathe. Rita will be late getting home, she thought, as if that were the main consideration. No wonder her father had found the Manor phones busy.

Alma Potter at large under cover of the storm. Alma Potter, now using two canes instead of a walker. Supposing it were just possibly so, how far could she get? And how fast?

Pam let out a wavering yip. "Here she is. That's her."

"Where?" Kirsty jerked around to scan the row of windows before she realized Pam was pointing to something in the paper.

It was a small, slightly fuzzy photograph on the inside back page. A person in what might be a wheelchair was being handed a large greeting card that said CONGRATULATIONS on the front.

Kirsty gave it a quick glance, then read the caption. "Thanksgiving Day will mark the 100th birthday of Frederiksen's first kindergarten teacher. Alma Potter, Custer Memorial Manor, credits her longevity to vitality soaked up from all those youngsters through the years. Of her birthday Potter says, 'If I make it past my first hundred, I'll start planning for the second.' "

"I didn't know that was her," Pam marveled. "She looked just ordinary. She even smiled at me."

"She smiled at you? Alma Potter? Where? When?"

"At the gift shop Saturday. A girl was taking pictures of her in the hall—a photographer. Daddy saw her, too."

Kirsty returned her eyes cautiously to the old face in the photo. Besides the photo's poor quality, the newsprint was smeary. There wasn't much she could be sure of. Were those eyes slyly hooded or merely sunken and puffy? Was that a smirking grin or part of the big bow under the old woman's chin? It had to be purely her imagination that detected something eerily familiar behind the inky smudge.

"That's Mrs. Vohl," Pam said, tapping the hand extending in from the edge of the photo to touch the card. "She was trying not to show."

Mrs. Vohl really did get around. The thought gave a lurch to the queasiness that was starting to roll in Kirsty's stomach.

The phone began ringing.

"Maybe it's your mom," she said hopefully. She would be as glad as Pam to have Rita home, she discovered.

Pam scrambled out of the chair and ran to answer. Kirsty heard her eager, "Hello," followed in a moment by one less confident. "Hello?"

There was a long silence. Kirsty wheeled into the hall. Pam was staring blankly at the wall, the receiver against her ear.

"Who is it?' Kirsty asked.

98

"I don't know. It's just humming. Like someone whispering, sort of."

"There must be trouble on the line. Hang up," Kirsty said, and shivered. Any minute she expected to see her breath turn to frost in here. Yet she had shoved the thermostat up to 80.

Pam lowered the receiver. Almost at once the phone started ringing again. She backed away, hands clasped behind her. "You answer."

Kirsty put the receiver to her ear and listened. No humming now. No sound at all for a space of seconds.

"Hello?" she said.

A throat cleared itself. "Did you know your cat's locked in Mrs. Vohl's car in her garage?"

"What? Who is this?"

"Your cat's locked in Mrs. Vohl's car."

She knew who it was by now. "That's not funny, Alf Thayer. You get off this line and quit playing games with our phone."

She banged the receiver down.

The Golden Oldie, "Winter Wonderland," coming from the radio stopped abruptly. All the lights went out.

9

THERE WAS ENOUGH light from outdoors that the house was not plunged into absolute darkness, but it took Kirsty a moment to adjust to the change from full brightness to deep twilight. She expected a wail or an exclamation from Pam, but Pam was leaning against the wall, head tilted, eyes half shut, as if she were miles away in thought and hadn't noticed a thing. In fact, her expression was very like Mrs. Vohl's when Kirsty had imagined her hearing messages on a private receiver.

"Hey, wake up," she said, and was chagrined to hear a shake in her voice. "Are you falling asleep or what?"

Pam didn't stir from her trance except to produce a vacant smile. "I know who was whispering on the phone."

"It was trouble on the line," Kirsty said loudly, as if it were necessary to have that fact established throughout the house. "Or else it was Alf Thayer trying to be smart and scare us."

"It was her. It was the witch," Pam crooned. "She knows we're here. She's coming for us."

"Stop that." Kirsty grabbed her by the arm and shook her. "Stop it. I don't want to hear any more about witches."

Pam goggled at her, owl-eyed in the dimness, her mouth ajar. Was she turning again into yesterday's remote-controlled zombie?

Kirsty gave her another shake. "Where's Toby?" The answer to that seemed all at once vital. For his sake, she told herself. Because she wanted to be sure he was okay.

"Toby?" Pam sounded as if she had never heard the name.

"Toby," Kirsty shouted at her. "Your cat. You said maybe he's upstairs. Go find him."

Pam jerked free of her, understanding beginning to firm the slack lines of her face. Understanding—and fear. "The lights are all off. It's dark."

"Because the power went off," Kirsty said. "It's not that dark. You can still see."

And the lights might come back on at any minute, she reminded herself. It was just a temporary, run-of-the-mill power outage, nothing more.

She started toward her own room. Sometimes Toby liked to stretch at his ease on her pillows. What a laugh she would have on Alf if Toby were peacefully napping there now.

She cut the corner too short going through her door. The crunch of her knuckles between the door jamb and her wheel brought her to a wincing stop.

Pressing her bruised fingers to her mouth, she stared at the bed. There was no sign of a cat, not even a dent where a cat might have been.

She eased forward, straining to see into the shadows. He had to be somewhere. He was seldom far away.

The silver frame of the photograph beside her bed was a dull gleam in the half-light. She could hardly make out the figures inside the frame, grouped in that safe, happy circle that should never have been broken. Her eyelids smarted with tears prompted by more than the pain in her hand.

"What's that smell?" Pam asked behind her.

"What smell?" Kirsty sniffed, and the hairs on the back of her neck prickled. There was only a trace of odor in the air and she had smelled it only once before, but she knew that smell of something rotten burning.

"Is that the witch smell?" Pam whispered. "Is she coming?"

"Why aren't you looking for Toby? What are you doing in here?"

"I don't want to be alone in the dark."

The dark was, in fact, growing deeper by the second. Kirsty's bed, her dresser, her desk were little more now than objects without form.

"Go get a flashlight or something," she said desperately.

"I don't know where there is one," Pam whimpered. "You do something. You're the oldest."

"Do something like what?" Kirsty asked.

She had never thought of herself as "the oldest," not in the sense of taking charge and being the responsible one. That was always Gail's role. Kirsty was the one who followed or else goofed off and got away with it because she was younger. Gail had been thirteen years old, after all.

Thirteen. The same age as Kirsty now. Why hadn't it struck her before that she was as old as Gail?

She flinched as a peal of thunder rumbled outside. She wasn't ready to be "the oldest." She didn't want to be.

The room was lit by a glare of lightning. Thunder and lightning in a snowstorm? The flash was not as brilliant as in a summer storm, but it served to show her that the sly look was creeping across Pam's face again.

"I know where there's some matches," Pam said, starting to sidle by her. "We could light this candle—"

"No." Kirsty lurched to snatch the tree candle from the dresser before Pam reached it. "I don't care how dark it gets."

"How am I going to find Toby?" The tone was wheedling, not fearful.

Kirsty tucked the candle behind her in the chair. The smell in the room was growing stronger. She tried a deep breath to hold down her jumpy nerves. Instead, it made her head spin.

"Maybe you can't find him. Maybe he never got back

in after you threw him out this morning. Alf Thayer says he's locked in Mrs. Vohl's car in her garage. That's what he just told me on the phone."

"I threw Toby out?" Pam said it as if this were the first she had heard of it. "I didn't. I wouldn't. I—" She faltered, and finished on a sob. "I didn't want to. I couldn't help it. I tried, but I couldn't help it."

She whirled and ran into the hall, crying and calling "Toby! Toby!"

Kirsty thought unexpectedly of Mrs. Vohl crying about the bad things she did but unable to remember doing them. What else might Pam have done and forgotten while no one was here to stop her? What might she be going to do next?

Matches, popped into Kirsty's head. Pam knew where there were matches—

"Wait," Kirsty called, starting after her. "Wait."

She heard Pam stumbling up the stairs in the dark. Then she saw a glow in the living room. This time there could be no mistake. The shifting light was firelight.

"Pam," she tried to shout, but she couldn't drag air enough into her lungs for more than a squawk.

"I'll find him," Pam answered from upstairs. "I'll find him. Toby—"

Kirsty turned the corner into a wash of firelight and shadow. The far window blazed with blue-tipped red and yellow flames. But they were not a reflection. There was no fire on the real hearth to reflect.

Part of Kirsty wanted to back off fast, but another part held her motionless, unable to tear her gaze away. Hadn't she yearned to see that other room again? It was like yearning to see Santa Claus in person when she was small, only to be petrified with terror when he actually appeared.

Pain jumped in her head, like someone jerking on a chain fastened between her eyes. She automatically inched forward to ease the pull. It helped, and she inched forward farther. And farther. By the time she had traveled across the room to the window, the pain had given way to a delicious lightness as if she could float on air.

Footsteps thudded overhead. Far off Pam was still calling Toby.

"Never mind that," murmured a voice in Kirsty's head that was not Kirsty's. "It's nothing to do with you."

The flames on the other hearth cast a dancing brightness over every part of the room, promising warmth and cheer in contrast to the chill shadows of the room where she sat. Highlights played along the paneled door, which now stood nearly wide open and directly in front of her. In the room beyond it, she could make out not only the flowered couch but the person sitting on it and another person, less distinct, leaning over her shoulder.

Recognition burst on her like a rocket. Her mother. And Gail.

They were posed as they were in the photograph, smiling at her, waiting for her, wanting her to join them. All she need do was cross over the windowsill to their side.

She would be able to walk again, to run, jump, do anything.

But how did she cross the sill of the window that could not be opened?

Upstairs there was a slam, a thump, a cry: "Kirsty—"

"Forget her," the voice murmured. "She's all right. She's always all right."

The open door looked close enough to touch. If she could just reach through the glass and grasp that doorknob. The voice urged her on. "Go ahead. You can do it."

She could do it. She could cross through to that other side and stand up, glad and tall, the way she used to be. Her fingers closed on the doorknob.

A pretty far step down on the other side . . . Who was it who had once said that? Pam?

Somewhere far off a little kid was crying hysterically. The sound was all but drowned by a roar like wind in Kirsty's ears. Cold wind. Colder than the chill room she was about to leave. Why didn't she feel heat from those lively flames on the hearth?

Her mother and Gail went on smiling encouragement at her.

"This is your chance," the voice prompted. "Take it."

The little kid crying was Pam. She was in a panic for some reason. She needed help.

"Hurry." The voice carried a trace of impatience. "Your one chance. Run with it."

Or stay in a wheelchair forever. There were no other

choices. There was, in fact, no choice at all. Kirsty gathered herself for the lunge that would lift her onto the sill and over the edge.

"Kirsty, help. Help me—" The cry was weaker, fading. Pam was not all right.

Kirsty's hand loosened its grip on the doorknob, but she couldn't pull it free. Her fingers seemed stuck to the ice-cold knob as if they were frozen there.

"Yes!" The voice was no longer just inside her head. It pulsed in the air around her. Her wrist felt as if steely fingers had closed around it.

"She's mine," the voice snarled at her. "The little one's already mine. You can't save her. Now *you* come." A sharp tug wrenched at Kirsty's wrist. "I want you both. I've been too long without."

"No." Kirsty fought against the unbelievable force that began to drag her onto the windowsill. Her free hand beat against her captive wrist with no effect. She clutched at her chair and tried to force it backward. A lamp cord snaked out, tangling in her wheel and bringing the lamp down with a crash.

Her mother and Gail continued to smile their fixed, uninvolved smiles at her. What was wrong with them? Why were they letting this happen? Why didn't they rise up and come to her aid?

Something hard was digging into her hip. The tree candle. It was crowded down behind her where she had stuffed it out of reach of Pam. Her cherished tree candle, Gail's last gift to her. The big, bulky, solid candle.

She grasped it by its stubby trunk and swung it like a club at the door whose knob was holding her fast. The candle slammed against the beckoning fire on that other hearth and flew backward from her hand to land somewhere behind her near the real fireplace.

Her mother and Gail shimmered along with the fire on that hearth. Then all vanished in a rain of shattered glass, and the grip on her wrist was broken, too.

10

"LITTLE FOOL," the witch voice hissed through the jagged break in a pane. "All the worse for you."

Kirsty rubbed her throbbing wrist. Snow-peppered wind gusted in through the gap in the glass, freshening her mind as well as the air she was breathing. The living room was murky with smoke, she realized.

She yanked frantically at the lamp cord to clear her wheel.

"Not so fast," the witch voice cried.

The carpet began to ripple under Kirsty's chair, lifting first one wheel, then the other, threatening to spill her overboard. She pushed on the wheels with all her might to back away from the window.

A thought flashed through her head. Maybe the witch wasn't all-powerful. There was one thing she feared. "Toby," Kirsty gasped. Perhaps he was nowhere within earshot, but it was worth a try. She gulped air into her lungs and called at the top of her voice, "Toby! Here, Toby. Come, kitty, kitty. Come, Toby."

"Very clever, my dear," the witch voice mocked. "But he won't come."

The carpet heaved in a broad billow beneath Kirsty. She hung on fiercely to the chair arms, but it was no use. The chair pitched forward, and she was falling, plummeting down into chill and empty blackness.

A scream from outside broke her fading consciousness: "Cat!"

Kirsty hit the floor hard, and the overturned chair crashed down heavily on top of her. For a minute or more she just lay there, listening to the sudden stillness everywhere.

Something thudded onto the windowsill. She was afraid to twist her head to look, but she made herself do it. The silhouette of a cat crouched there, peering in.

"Toby?" she whispered, not quite trusting her eyes.

He sprang into the room with a questioning mew that suggested he was no less astonished to find her flattened under an upended chair. She stretched a hand to him and felt the furry reality of his cheek against it. Did this mean they were safe now? That the witch had fled?

Toby sneezed, and she grew aware again of the smoke in the air.

Pam. Where was Pam? The witch had told her to forget about Pam, and she had done exactly that.

Wind wheezing in past the remnants of glass in the

window hissed like a taunting snicker. Otherwise the house was silent.

Toby growled in the depths of his throat and laid his ears back. He sank to his belly and glided toward the hallway and the stairs.

Kirsty hitched her elbows under her and began painfully to writhe out from under her chair. At once the old, warning ache struck her between the eyes. If the witch had fled, she had not gone far.

Kirsty clenched her teeth against the ache and rolled clear of the chair. She kept on rolling into the hall and on to the foot of the stairs. She half expected the carpet to lift in another billow to stop her, but the floors stayed flat and firm beneath her all the way.

She sat up, a little dizzy and surprisingly short of breath. It took her several gasps before she could shout up the stairs, "Pam? Where are you?"

Toby was up there somewhere, mewing. It sounded as if he were also rattling a doorknob. She had seen him do that, jumping up and down to protest a shut door. He hated shut doors.

"Pam? Are you okay?" she shouted a trifle louder. "Where are you?"

Maybe she was hiding in one of the bedrooms, or had locked herself in the bathroom. It would be so simple if Kirsty could just run up these stairs and see.

"You can't save her," the voice had said. Was that what it meant? That Kirsty was out of it so far as anything happening upstairs was concerned?

Well, maybe the voice was mistaken.

Kirsty planted her hands behind her and hoisted herself to a seat on the bottom step. After a second to rest, she pulled herself up to the next step.

The third step was harder. Her feet were off the floor now, and she was dragging her full weight upward. Still, she made it. And the fourth step. The fifth. The sixth . . .

Her shirt was clammy with perspiration when she rested, panting, on the landing, four steps short of the top. Her ears were buzzing. Then she heard something snapping.

She looked over her shoulder to see fireworks going off outside a window at the head of the stairs. Blue-white sparks were arching and spitting across an angle of the roof, where they were melting a black track through the layers of snow.

Kirsty's bones became jelly. This was no cheap magic trick done with reflections. This had to be a fallen power line—the same high-voltage line that had set the house on fire the day it went up for sale and had nearly done so the day the Hamiltons moved in. What if the house burst into flames now? She was midway up the stairs and an impossible distance from any chance of escape.

"Pam," she shouted into the upper hall. "Pam?" She could smell scorching wood somewhere. "Pam, wherever you are, come out. The house is burning."

Something thudded feebly against a wall or a closed door above her.

Her effort to call again was choked off by a coughing fit. The smoke she had noted in the living room was thickening up here, too. And she was so tired. Very likely she and Pam were a lost cause no matter what she did, so why struggle further?

As she thought it, her hands were behind her and her elbows straightening to haul her up the next step.

Toby met her at the top. He rubbed himself against her shoulder, purring, then raced off to mew in front of a shut door. The sparks flickering outside shed light enough for her to see him and to see that none of the other four doors opening off the hall was shut.

The dark closet, she remembered. The one where the door sticks. Hadn't she known it all along?

It was the second door on the left, and it looked a mile away. She would have to crawl to get there. The hall was too narrow for her to lie down and roll.

Her head was pounding like a drumbeat as she passed the first door, the bathroom. An array of angry sparks was framed by the window in there, too.

The display in both windows grew wilder and brighter the closer she inched to the closet. Why didn't somebody in the neighborhood see them and phone the fire department or the police?

She had a giddy moment of seeing the closet doorknob change to a ball of hissing sparks. Toby reared up and slapped at the jagged flashes as if they were bugs climbing the wall. Instantly they shrank to an ordinary knob again. Kirsty grabbed it quickly and twisted before her courage could desert her completely. She threw her weight into an outward tug, expecting the door to resist. Instead, it opened as easily as a book and sent her sprawling on her back.

Smoke and rotten witch smell poured over her. A wad of crumpled paper like an overgrown spitball spun out of the air and struck her cheek with cutting force. She scarcely noted it as she scrambled to sit up and peer into the closet.

It was a big closet, as big as a very small room. The blackness inside seemed to go on forever. Nothing stirred in it.

"Pam?"

Still no movement, no sound. Her hand exploring into the darkness touched a sweater, an arm, five small, limp fingers spread on the floor. The fingers were clammy and cold and made no response when she squeezed them.

She couldn't tell if Pam were even breathing. Somehow she had to get her downstairs and out where there was fresh air.

She pulled and tugged her as far as the bathroom. There a snarl from Toby stopped her. She heard a faint crackling behind her like tiny, mocking laughter.

Turning, she saw the wad of paper that had struck her. It was slowly unfolding into a sheet of drawing paper— an all-too-familiar sheet. The edges were tattered and smudged, but the witch face was bold and sharp as ever. Its grin radiated a glow of its own.

114

Sudden fury swallowed Kirsty's fear. Would nothing ever destroy that horrible sketch?

She crushed the paper into a wad again and, scarcely taking aim, shot it back at the pale shadow that was the toilet. The wad landed in the bowl with a watery plop. At once the water began to fizz and churn. A cloud of vapor rose from it.

Kirsty flung herself forward to where she could grasp the flush lever and press it. By then the paper was only a few black flakes that swirled frantically like drowning beetles before they vanished down the drain.

As clear, clean water rushed in to fill the emptied bowl, there was a gigantic *pop* outdoors. The snapping sparks along the power line died as if a plug had been pulled.

In the same instant, the terrible aching in Kirsty's head stopped. It dissolved as if it had never been.

She groped her way back through the dark to the hall. A hand met hers and clasped it, a small, warm hand very much alive.

"Pam?" she gasped. "You're okay?" She wouldn't have believed she could feel so glad.

"I found Toby," Pam said in a voice scratchy from smoke.

In the stillness, Kirsty could hear the cat purring. She heard, too, a far-off wail of fire sirens—far off, but getting closer.

IT WAS CLOSE to noon the next day when the hospital pronounced Kirsty and Pam sufficiently recovered from smoke inhalation to go home.

Sun-warmed upholstery met Kirsty's shoulders when her father lifted her into the car. Rivers of meltwater were flowing along the gutters, glinting under a sky of sunlit blue.

Pam, scrambling in beside her, cast a puzzled glance around the bare pavement of the parking lot. "Where's all the snow?"

"Better look fast if you want to see any," Kirsty's father advised in the light tone he had been keeping up ever since his arrival at the hospital last night.

"That was the craziest storm," Rita said from the front seat. "One minute it was snowing and blowing a regular blizzard, and the next it just stopped dead. The wind died, the snow stopped, and the temperature started going up. That was just before I got the call that you girls were at the hospital, and when I went out to my car, the snow was melting off the streets already."

Kirsty fingered the woven band of her seat belt. Now was the moment to ask the question that had been lurking in her mind ever since the rescuing firemen carried her and Pam out of the house last night. She did not want to go back to that house without an answer. "The radio said someone from the nursing home got lost in the storm. That Alma Potter person. Did she ever get found?"

"Yes," Rita said slowly, "she was found, but it was too late. She was an old, old lady with a bad heart, and her heart gave out."

A bad heart, indeed, Kirsty thought. Her own heart did a small skip of relief.

"Where was she?" Pam asked.

Rita gave her head a wondering shake. "On the floor by her bed when they found her. Where she had been all the time before that while we were hunting high and low is anybody's guess. She was soaking wet."

Kirsty shut her eyes against the full glare of the sun as the car rounded a corner. Behind her lids she saw the crumpled witch sketch spinning down the drain on a rush of water. She could guess at an answer, but by the broad light of day, she wasn't sure she believed it any more than her father would if she told him.

The emergency room nurse had hushed Pam's efforts to tell of an invisible creature that tried to choke her in the closet. "You were spaced out on smoke fumes, honey," she said. "You had a bad dream."

The smoke had come from two foam-rubber cushions and a quantity of newspaper stuffed into the basement stove and lighted. Pam had only the haziest recollection of doing it, and no explanation beyond "I was so cold." It was the doctor's opinion that she might have been running a fever and been slightly out of her head yesterday afternoon. Everyone appeared satisfied to leave it at that. Perhaps Kirsty should be, too.

The car started up the hill to the house that was Alma Potter's no more. Kirsty pressed her cheek to the window, straining to see ahead. What she was looking for she was not sure until she caught the gleam of sun glancing off windows behind the front yard trees. Three gleams of light from three tall living room windows. Three. Not four.

"I broke that one front window," she said. No way was that anybody's dream. She also knew how she had done it and why. Believable or not, it had happened.

"We're pretty broad-minded about letting air in any way you can when the smoke gets too thick," her father said, piloting the car to a stop in the driveway. "Another few minutes in those fumes, the fire chief told me, and you'd have passed out. Some freak of the storm blew a trash bag across the chimney and froze it there. The smoke had no way to escape."

"If that wasn't enough, there was an electrical fire, too,

getting underway between the walls. When I think how things might have turned out—" Rita paused to blow her nose. Then she smiled over the back of the seat before she opened the door to get out. "We are four very lucky people."

Kirsty was surprised by the glow that spread through her in response, as if she had joined hands in a special circle.

She was surprised, too, by how good her chair felt under her when her father helped her into it. The control it gave her over where she moved and which restored her to an independence she had greatly undervalued until now. Last night had taught her that there were worse fates than coping with a wheelchair through the years ahead.

In the kitchen, Toby rose from his favorite cushion to welcome them by rubbing his head against the spindles of the chair back.

Pam went down on her knees to hug him. "Toby, Toby, Toby." A trace of color began to creep into her pale cheeks. "I was afraid maybe he would be so scared of all those firemen he might run away, but they wouldn't let me take him along."

"He spent the night at your friend Mrs. Vohl's," Kirsty's father said. "She took him home for safekeeping right after you girls were packed off to the hospital. She brought him back this morning."

Mrs. Vohl? Kirsty tried without success to fit her into

the confusion of sirens and trucks, blinding lights and swarming firemen that had ended last night's terror. Where had Mrs. Vohl been?

"She also brought us a pot of chili, which we are going to have for lunch," Rita said, pulling a large covered dish from the refrigerator. "Be sure to tell her how much we appreciated everything the next time you see her. She's such a good neighbor, and so upset by what happened here that you might think it was her doing."

Pam lifted her face from nuzzling Toby. Her gaze crossed with Kirsty's for the briefest of seconds. A spark jumped between them, a flicker of shared comprehension too quickly gone to identify.

Kirsty's father touched her shoulder. "Just so you're prepared, the firemen had to take a panel off the inside of your closet to get at the wiring. They didn't do too much serious damage—the fire was only some smoldering rubbish—but your room is a mess. There hasn't been time to put it back in order."

Smoldering rubbish? Was that all the witch smell would amount to in the end? "What kind of rubbish?"

"Building debris mostly, it looked like. Wood chips, scraps, wastepaper." Rita tasted the chili and reached for the spice drawer. "It seems there was some remodeling done before this house went on the market. They apparently closed up a closet that opened into the living room and added the space to make the bedroom one a decent size. One of the workmen must have decided the

120

easiest way to dispose of anything he had no use for was to stuff it out of sight behind his paneling."

Kirsty had no need to ask where the closed-up living room closet had been. She had seen the door. Her throat tightened against a spot still raw from smoke, and she was thrown into a fit of coughing.

"Hey, hey, take it easy." Her father nudged Rita aside to fill a glass of water at the sink. "Here." He put it into Kirsty's hand. "Cool the dramatics. We weren't going to send you back to school this afternoon anyway."

He used the same light tone as before, but when she glanced up to hand him the emptied glass, there were lines of concern at the corners of his eyes and he was not laughing. It was Kirsty who had to struggle against bursting into crazy laughter. After the terrors of last night, what was Viktor Tweeten Middle School?

"You could sleep in my room tonight if yours is too messy," Pam volunteered. "You don't have to just stay downstairs anymore. Right? Because, you know what?" The question was directed to the kitchen in general. "Kirsty got all the way upstairs all by herself last night to find me."

"Yes, we know." Rita's spoon dripped unheeded onto the stove as she turned to look at Kirsty. "But I doubt she's going to want to do that every day."

Kirsty gave her a weak grin, and resisted the impulse to flex her sore muscles. This morning she had been too stiff to move until the nurse had whisked her off to a

121

whirlpool treatment. Kirsty suspected the suggestion had come from Rita, but the effect was so deliciously soothing yet invigorating that it would be hard—maybe stupid—not to accept if the opportunity were ever offered again. She would have to think about that.

"And then we grabbed hands in the dark and slid downstairs together before the firemen got in," Pam continued, caught up in the spell of her own narration. "And then that one dumb fireman wouldn't even believe us when we told him."

"That shows he doesn't know Kirsty," Gene Hamilton said. This time his grin was real.

Kirsty ran her hand down the length of Toby's back. He arched himself, purring, and rubbed his cheek against her fingers. She knew exactly how he felt.

He jumped down and padded along behind her, followed by Pam, to view the condition of her room.

The room was a disaster. Clothes lay strewn across the bed just as they had been pulled from her closet and tossed. The closet curtain was shoved to one side as far as it would go, and a width of splintered paneling leaned beside a gap in the rear wall. A gritty, dark trail of plaster dust and smudged ashes marked the firemen's route across the carpet.

The framed photograph sat in its place on the bedside table, but a diagonal crack ran the length of it from one corner to the other.

Someone—her father or Rita—had rescued the tree candle from wherever it had landed last night in the living room and had leaned it against the mirror on the dresser. The candle was cracked, too, across its branches, and it wobbled when she tried to stand it upright on its base.

Pam was inspecting the hole in the closet. "There's something still in here," she reported, fishing up a grubby looking rag. "Somebody's purple sock."

"That's not purple. It's lavender, like Mrs. Vohl always wears. Ugh! It smells." Kirsty turned her head from the musty, perhaps even mousy, odor of it. "Throw it out."

"No, wait. It's not a sock. It's a puppet. See?" Pam worked her hand into the thing and waggled her fingers. A crudely embroidered face bobbed and nodded above a prim little collar of crocheted lace that ended in a trailing crocheted chain like a leash.

"Ugly." Kirsty backed away from the thing, as repelled by its looks as she was by its smell. Something clicked in her brain. "I bet that's one of Alma Potter's puppets, the ones Mrs. Vohl said were on a shelf in the living room. That shelf could have been in that closet that got closed up." Wherever the shelf had been, one more souvenir of Alma Potter was not on her list of heart's desires. "Go stuff it in the trash."

"The puppets were storybook people," Pam remembered. "This one is—" She squinted at a small tag under the lace collar. "Z-E-L-D-A. Zelda. Did you ever hear of that name?"

Kirsty could not recall that she had, but it started her on another odd train of thought. Suppose this was how the witch kept control of those in her power, her familiars—by giving a puppet the same name and making it act out what she wanted done.

"Will you please just get rid of that thing?"

"Okay, okay." Pam danced the puppet along the foot of the bed, heading in the direction of the door, but also in the direction of Toby, settled on Kirsty's down vest amid the tumble of clothes. Toby's paw shot out and snagged the dangling crocheted cord as it went by. Pam, startled, jerked it the other way. The string of chain stitches raveled swiftly up its length and into the collar. The little collar twitched and fell to pieces.

Without the collar to shape and define it, the face as swiftly flattened and the embroidered features took on the appearance of haphazard darns.

"Look what you did," Pam scolded, half-laughing, half-amazed. "You raveled Zelda's leash and let her get away."

"Girls," Rita called from the kitchen. "Lunch."

"Coming." Pam set off at a trot, the lavender rag still on her hand.

Kirsty delayed for one more attempt to stand the tree candle upright. Then she did what she had been trying not to do. She let herself look at the photograph.

A photograph. That was all it was now. Flat images on a flat oblong of treated paper.

She tilted it to various angles, searching for the sense of depth she had always found in it, the illusion that it was a window requiring only the proper key to open and welcome her inside. They were no longer there.

"Kirsty, lunch is ready," her father said from the doorway. He came to look over her shoulder. "Don't worry about that. The man from Frank's Glass will be here to fit the front window. We'll have him cut a new piece of glass to fit that frame, too."

Like the lid to Snow White's coffin, Kirsty thought. Only in time Snow White had been restored, alive and well, to those who loved her. Gail and her mother were never coming back. In her heart of hearts she had never absolutely believed that until now.

She ran her thumbnail along the slanting crack that had somehow let the life inside the frame evaporate. "I could have gone with them," she murmured, remembering how tempted she had been by that last, sweetest, and most deadly sugarplum the witch had offered.

Her father took the photograph from her hands. "Don't fiddle with that. You'll damage the picture, and we don't have too many of the four of us together. Somebody had to be on the other end of the camera."

Surprise brought her head up. "Do you mean we still have other pictures?" She had never asked because she had assumed she knew the answer.

"Boxes. They're downstairs in a trunk with the other keepsakes."

Keepsakes, too? She wanted to ask what they were, which memories from their old home he had saved. But the list could wait. More important was the fact that he had kept them.

"Daddy—" She studied her hands in her lap. "Do you think about them sometimes? About Mama and Gail?"

"I think about them." He set the photograph down in front of her. "You remind me of your mother so often."

"Me? Gail—"

"Gail had her coloring, but you have her temperament, a lot of her fire. She would have done exactly as you did last night under the same circumstances, and never thought about it twice. She would be proud of you."

He could not have given Kirsty higher praise, yet when she brushed at a tickle on her cheek, her hand came away wet with tears. Part of her that had been numb for a long time was starting to throb, starting to ache. No more could she pretend that behind the next door she opened, inside the next window she passed, around the next corner she turned, Gail and her mother might be waiting. They would not.

"Daddy—" The word was a hard knot in her throat. "When I said that about calling Pam Gail, I didn't mean it against Gail. I wasn't saying—"

"I know. I figured it out afterward. And Rita told me, too."

He sat on the edge of the bed beside her chair. "Don't ever doubt that I am on your side, whatever. I admit to maybe being hasty in my judgments at times. But sometimes so are you. You're my daughter, too, you know."

Quickly, awkwardly, he bent and hugged her.

12

THE AFTERGLOW of that hug was still a soft warmth around Kirsty when she braved the living room later that afternoon. She was braced for mental replays of last night to be waiting for her, although the room had been set to rights as much as possible. The lamp that had tangled its cord in her wheel was back on its lamp table, its shade only a little crooked. The shards of jagged glass had been removed from the window frame, and a summerlike breeze wafting through it was clearing every vestige of smoke from the air.

The fact was that, far from being a place of chilling reminders, the room was more bright and airy and serene than she had ever known it. Something angry and brooding had gone out of the atmosphere.

Part of the new brightness was easily explained. The storm or the fallen power line had sheared off several big

127

branches from the trees in the yard. She could actually see a good-sized stretch of the road in either direction.

As she watched, a flame-red car whizzed past, going down the hill, and sped out of sight. She heard it growl as it slowed at the lower corner. Then there it was again. flashing up the hill and into the Hamilton driveway.

"Rita," her father called, loud enough to be heard above the vacuum humming in Kirsty's room. "Pam, Kirsty. Company."

Kirsty was already on her way to the kitchen. There, in the center of the table, sat a magnificent poinsettia. What might be a human poinsettia stood behind it, wearing green and yellow checked pants and a red jacket with white piping.

"I apologize for rushing the season, bringing a Christmas decoration two days before Thanksgiving," the person was telling Kirsty's father, "but I won't be here to deliver it at the proper time. I just stopped in to say good-bye."

It was Mrs. Vohl. Kirsty had to concentrate on the gold foil crimped around the flower pot to keep from staring. Mrs. Vohl—with green eye shadow and bright lipstick, without a dot of lavender to be seen on her anywhere.

"You're going away for the holiday?" Rita asked.

Mrs. Vohl beamed. "Much longer than that. I handed my notice to the school this morning, effective immediately, put my house up for sale, bought myself some new clothes and new luggage, and I'm off to see the world."

At Rita's exclamation, she went on, "It's a dream I had even before Mr. Vohl passed away fifteen years ago, but there always seemed to be something holding me back. Then last evening it came over me all of a sudden that there was something about the garage I should remember but couldn't, something I might be sorry about if I didn't go check on it. So there I was knee-deep in snow, trying to wrestle my garage door open when the wind knocked me flat on my face just like someone had deliberately pushed me. Right then and there I decided I'd seen enough winter storms to last me a lifetime, and I couldn't think of a single good reason to stay here any longer, if I wanted to go."

"What about your garage?" Pam asked. "What was wrong with it?"

Mrs. Vohl looked vague a moment, then chuckled. "I haven't the least idea. By the time I picked myself up and dusted myself off, I was in such a state that I just left the door half-open and went back in the house to make plans."

She insisted that everyone troop outside to offer an opinion on the red car she was test-driving. Even to Kirsty, no expert on autos, it spoke of speed and style and sportiness—a creation light years removed from the subdued and serviceable white minivan.

"Don't you love the color?" Mrs. Vohl demanded. "I'm

done with pale and practical forever." She laughed, running a finger around the open collar of her shirt. "I think I know how a dog feels that slips its leash and collar and takes off running."

"Oh, dear." She clucked at a splash of mud on the fender. "Is there a rag handy?"

Pam ran to fetch one, and Mrs. Vohl wiped earnestly.

"I wish I could take you all for a spin," she said, sliding onto the low seat behind the wheel, "but there's room for only one passenger at a time, and I'm overdue getting back to the dealer." She waved as the engine roared. "Happy holidays. I won't forget you. I hope you'll think kindly of Zelda Vohl sometimes, too."

The car shot backward down the drive, did a squealing turn at the street, and zoomed off down the hill.

""What did she say?" Kirsty asked.

"That she couldn't offer us a ride. Thank goodness," Rita said.

She and Kirsty's father went back in the house, but Kirsty and Pam were slower to move from the pleasant heat of the sun radiating off the pavement.

"What did you do with that Zelda puppet?" Kirsty asked.

"She took it with her. That's the rag I gave her to wipe the car."

They looked at each other, not speaking. Kirsty's thoughts tumbled over one another. Mrs. Vohl, who had a nightmare that she was a puppet forced to do someone else's will— It was Mrs. Vohl who had provided a purse for Pam's tooth and the means by which it was lost; Mrs. Vohl who had kept Kirsty separate and lonely at school and seen to it that Pam and Kirsty were isolated beyond assistance during the storm; Mrs. Vohl who had fits of weeping over bad things she had done, yet could never remember what they were. Like locking Toby in her garage for a crucial hour or two perhaps. Zelda Vohl as a little girl had run errands for Alma Potter. Had she, without quite realizing it, never been allowed to stop?

Pam's green eyes were wide with the same questions. "The witch made her do things," she breathed. "Do you think?"

Slowly, Kirsty nodded and turned a tiny shiver into a shrug.

"Hey, Peanut," came a hail from the street. Alf and Dean Thayer were cruising down the hill on their bikes. As usual, they were hugging the far side of the street as they neared the Hamiltons' house.

"There's nobody here called that," Pam shouted back.

The boys stopped opposite the driveway. "Okay, Peanut *Face*," Dean said, and snickered. "I thought your house burned down, Peanut Face."

"Well, it didn't," Pam flung at him. "And no witches got us, either. That old witch woman is dead."

"Old Lady Potter?" Alf swerved to a halt in the middle of the street, one foot on the center line.

"She's dead," Kirsty said. "So you don't have to be scared anymore. You can cross the street."

Alf's red, chapped face took on a deeper red. "Who

131

said I was scared? Do you think I believe in all that witch garbage?"

Dean slid off his bike close to his brother. "Yeah, we could cross this street a hundred times a day if we wanted."

"Oh?" A soft breeze ruffled Kirsty's hair, and she was aware of how lovely it was to be comfortably warm once again, right down to her toes. "What about your cousin Lisa?"

Alf curled his upper lip like a TV villain expressing scorn. "Did I ever say I believed her? I only told you what she said."

"They're just mad because they can't scare us anymore," Pam said.

Kirsty narrowed her eyes, watching Alf. Believer or not, a dose of his own medicine wouldn't hurt. "They don't know what we know."

"Like what we found behind the wall in the closet," Pam suggested.

"Like what?" Dean demanded at once. "Not witch stuff."

Pam opened her mouth to answer, but Kirsty laid a hand on her arm. "Don't tell them."

They locked glances, she and Pam, and this time the communication between them was no fleeting spark, no mere flash. It was an open line.

"Just be careful you don't get us too mad," she advised the boys.

"This is dumb. I've got papers to deliver," Alf said, but

Kirsty didn't miss the uneasy roll of his eyes toward her and the house as he hitched himself back on his bike.

"You're a pile of garbage, Peanut," Dean said, turning to follow Alf.

"Her name is Pam," Kirsty said sweetly. "It might be wise to remember that."

Dean hunched over his handlebars, peddling to pick up speed. "Pam, Pam, Pam—What do I care, anyway. That's even a dumber name than Peanut."

Pam and Kirsty were still giggling over their triumph when they entered the kitchen minutes later. Let the Thayers chew a while on the possibility that she and Pam might have inherited a degree of unnatural power from the house's former owner, Kirsty thought. It might even be true, considering this strange bond of telepathy that was developing between her and Pam. She had no idea if it would last or fade away as mysteriously as it came, but for the time being, a bond it was, such as she had never known with Gail or any other human being.

Rita was at the kitchen table, the battered tree candle in front of her. "I've been studying this," she told Kirsty. "If we drilled a small hole up through the center and inserted a long nail, we might get it to stand steady on its bottom again."

Kirsty took the candle. Rita seemed to have a knack for seeing things and understanding, like that business about Pam and Gail, and now the importance of this candle.

"I'll get it," Pam yipped as the phone began to ring.

She dodged past Kirsty and around the table in a sprint for the hall. Obviously, extraordinary new powers had not altered the basic Pam.

Odd that Kirsty should find that rather reassuring as she turned the candle over in her hands. Odd, too, to think she had been able to save Pam last night because Gail, through this gift, had saved her.

"Kirsty, it's for you," Pam reported, reappearing. "Some girl."

A girl here in Frederiksen calling her? Kirsty schooled herself not to sound too eager or hopeful when she lifted the receiver.

"Hi, this is Amber Lowry," the girl said. "I'm in your English class at school."

Amber, the girl who had talked to her yesterday, or tried to until Mrs. Vohl shooed her away.

"My dad's about to drive over to your place to measure a window—he's Frank's Glass," Amber went on. "I thought if it's okay I'd ride along and bring you the handout sheets Mrs. Morton gave us today. It's stuff we're supposed to read over Thanksgiving. She's big on giving vacation homework."

Kirsty groaned and they both laughed.

"By the way," Amber asked after giving her a rundown of what the work would be, "who was that who answered the phone? She sounds cute."

Kirsty weighed "cute," and decided that, within limitations, it might apply. "That's Pam."

"Who?"

Kirsty hunted for a term that would serve without complicated explanations. Somewhere inside her a door finished quietly closing to keep her big sister's memory safe; another door began slowly to open. "She's my— my little sister."

Rita had set the poinsettia on the stereo cabinet in the living room. Its vivid Christmas colors blazed out through the archway, proclaiming the season.

Kirsty made herself pause to look as she started back to the kitchen. Last night she had chosen to stay on this side of the dividing line, in this world where Christmas would be coming around again once every year, and where year by year she would gradually grow older than Gail and leave her behind.

There was no denying that the poinsettia was a rich, dramatic accent in the room. The dark green of her tree candle—her Christmas tree candle—would look nice beside it, she thought, as she moved on.

BEVERLY BUTLER, a native of Milwaukee, Wisconsin, lost her sight at fourteen. She began writing stories partly for typing practice so she could rejoin her high school class. Her classic *Light a Single Candle*, which won the Clara Ingram Judson Award, and *Gift of Gold* are both based on her experiences. *Witch's Fire*, her newest novel, is in no way based on personal experience, she says, although a distant cousin claims to have traced one branch of the family back to the Salem witch trials.

Beverly Butler's novels *Feather in the Wind* and *My Sister's Keeper* were each awarded a Certificate of Merit by the State Historical Society of Wisconsin. A nonfiction book, *Maggie by My Side*, was designated an American Library Association Notable Book. The Wisconsin Library Association has named her to its roster of notable Wisconsin writers.

She is married to T. V. Olsen, also a writer. They live in Rhinelander, Wisconsin, with a variety of interesting cats and dogs.